THE HADFIELD SERIES

Revealing a Rogue

Tempting a Gentleman

Loving a Dowager

First Edition October 2020

Developmental Edit by Gray Plume Editing

Edited by Rare Bird Editing

Proofread by Jennie Ladd and Magnolia Author Services

Cover design by The Swoonies Book Covers

Copyright © 2020 by Rachel Ann Smith

ISBN 978-1-951112-10-3

REVEALING A ROGUE

RACHEL ANN SMITH

PENFORD
PUBLISHING

*T*he big, black lettering on the placard next to the front door stopped Landon Neale, Earl of Hadfield, in his tracks. Unmoving, he stared at the sign. *Neale & Sons.*

Life was full of twists and turns.

During his formative years, the possibility of Landon inheriting the earldom had been remote. Both his uncle and cousin were hale and exhibited no signs of the lung condition that resulted in his papa's early death. Yet two years ago, he found himself thrust into the role of the Earl of Hadfield. A near-bankrupt estate was not all he had inherited; a generations-old duty to protect the royal family also accompanied the title. His days as a barrister and principal of his papa's law firm were in the past. Shrugging away the onset of melancholy, Landon pushed open the front door of the offices his papa left to him and his brother Christopher. Followed by the curious stares of the staff, he made his way down the hall. Duty dictated it was time for him to marry and produce an heir or two.

He hadn't visited his office or seen the woman he wished to propose to in nearly two years. Landon's heart skipped a beat. Anticipating the smell of old, musty books and files, Landon entered his office. He came to an abrupt halt in the middle of the room. His forehead contracted into a frown. On top of his desk, three neatly stacked bundles of files sat next to a vase filled with a white and pink floral arrangement. His brother had made no mention of another using his workspace. Landon glanced at the flowers—daisies. His lips twitched and then formed a smile. Miss Bronwyn, his former secretary, favored the blossoms. Perfect. If this was her workspace now, he wouldn't have to hunt the woman down.

Graham Drummond, Lord Archbroke, his cousin by marriage, had advised, "Best to be comfortable when proposing." Landon removed his greatcoat and hat. Glancing about the room, he placed them upon the chair his clients had once occupied. He patted the left side of his chest, and the crinkle of parchment settled his nerves. The special license Landon had asked Graham to procure sat securely inside his breast coat pocket.

Pacing in front of his desk, he mumbled, "Miss Bronwyn—" He paused. Brow furrowed, he searched his memory for her surname. *Good lord, how had he allowed the impropriety?* It was one thing not to be a stickler about such things but quite another to never have inquired in the six years she had acted as his personal secretary. He remembered quite distinctly Christopher introducing her as Miss Bronwyn, and he never questioned the familiarity of the introduction until now. The woman had inched her way into his heart and every thought, yet he hadn't a clue what Bronwyn's surname was. He'd have to rectify the oversight immediately. Otherwise, he couldn't formally propose to the woman. Landon chuckled and resumed pacing.

If his cousin Theo, Lady Archbroke, were here, she'd bemoan his lack of preparation. As a former barrister, he should be ashamed of himself, not knowing all the particulars regarding the woman he intended to tie himself to for life. Theo had provided every detail he could possibly need or want to know about each titled lady his mother had recommended to be the next Countess of Hadfield. Any of the delightful debutantes would have sufficed, but his heart belonged to one woman—Bronwyn. Granted, he didn't know her last name, nor her exact age, but those facts were of little consequence. The woman was intelligent, trustworthy, and excelled at challenging him. She was a mistress of rebuttals, and her expressive face captivated him. As head of the Protectors of the Royal Family, lovingly referred to as PORFs by its network of loyal supporters, Landon should have investigated Bronwyn's background before proposing. Still, she was the only woman he instinctively trusted to bear his heir. His son would inherit the title of earl but also bear the mark of a PORF as every other Earl of Hadfield had for ten generations.

His mind was set on making Miss Bronwyn the next Countess Hadfield and wife to the head PORF. Pausing at the window, he swept back the heavy drapes with the back of his hand and peered out onto the street. He missed watching her march up the street every morning. Her determined stride, combined with her distracted muttering, made for a delightful image.

The door swung open. His wandering thoughts vanished at the sight of her.

One of her hands remained on the door handle while the other held up a parchment covering her face. He smiled at the sharp tip of a black lead protruding from her walnut-brown hair. For years, he'd imagined himself snatching the pencil from Bronwyn's haphazard bun, releasing her locks, and threading his fingers through. He'd never dared while she was in his employ, nor had he risked touching her by wiping away the adorable graphite smudges that normally adorned her cheek.

Bronwyn released the door and strode into the room, her pretty features still hidden behind the file. Her skirts swirled around her legs, exposing the barest glimpse of her ankles.

"Of all the irresponsible…" she muttered.

Landon chuckled at her comment.

Bronwyn froze. "Oh! Lord Hadfield." Her cheeks reddened. "What are you doing here?"

Oh, how he missed Bronwyn's straightforward speech—her inability to lie and her propensity to get straight down to matters.

Clearing his throat, Landon replied, "Miss Bronwyn, it's a pleasure to be in your company again." He tilted his head, smiling.

"Revealing that roguish dimple of yours will not distract me. Explain your purpose, my lord."

He suppressed the urge to cup her face and bring her lips to his. Her sharp tongue incited fantasies of enjoying her fiery nature in his bed. "You think of me as a rogue?"

She gracefully turned around, ignoring his question, placing the parchment neatly upon the middle stack. In one fluid motion, she pulled back the chair and slid behind the desk. Only after she rested her forearms upon the wood and clasped her hands together did her gaze inch up to meet his. Struck by her sky-blue eyes, Landon stood mesmerized. Catching himself gaping at the woman like a besotted fool, he took a moment to take inventory of her features. Oh, it'd be no hardship, none at all, to look upon Bronwyn's sweet face every day.

Landon gestured to the middle stack. "What were you reading?"

Bronwyn leaned back and crossed her arms over her chest, settling them slightly below her modest décolleté. His concentration strayed—would her bosom fill the palm of his hand?

She gave him a *I know what you are thinking* look, and he promptly returned his gaze to hers.

"Why did you not answer my inquiry?" he asked.

Her answer was to wag both her eyebrows at him.

Landon took a step closer and leaned against the desk. "I didn't realize I needed a reason to visit *my* office."

"Mr. Neale reassigned *your* office to *me* since it appeared you no longer had use for it."

It was true his little brother no longer needed his help

nor his involvement in the running of the family business. Christopher had matters well in hand, while Landon was still coming to terms with the multitude of responsibilities he had inherited.

"My apologies, Miss Bronwyn. Christopher did not advise me of the change. Now, tell me, what could possibly have captured your attention to the extent you didn't notice my presence?"

"Lord Hadfield, I'm certain you're a very busy man. Please enlighten me as to the reason why you are here today."

The slight twitch of her fingertips was the only indication she wasn't entirely unaffected by his presence. Her bright blue eyes stunned him again into silence. In the past, he would have claimed that a brief or a case fact waylaid his thoughts. Now, he had no such pretenses to justify his behavior. Landon was one hundred percent obsessed with the woman who refused to give in and answer his questions first. His heart stopped at a slight up-tilt of Bronwyn's soft, kissable lips. Riveted by her alluring face... *What were they discussing?*

He gave his head a slight shake. He wasn't ready to reveal the true purpose for his appearance, yet the challenge in her gaze confirmed Landon's decision. Bronwyn was no blushing debutante seeking out a titled gentleman to care for her. No, Bronwyn could well fend for herself. While she may not need him, he needed her.

Bronwyn hadn't moved or fidgeted under his intense scrutiny. He grinned, producing his dimple once more.

Her eyes widened, but her lips thinned into a straight line.

For weeks he'd contemplated the risks of introducing a woman into the secret world of PORFs and the Network. He continued to ogle the woman who brazenly applied for the position of secretary and excelled in the role typically held by men. She was fearless. He had no doubts she would fully embrace and flourish in the clandestine role. Yes, Bronwyn would suit him well. The woman would not be swayed by a glare, nor a charming smile. Qualities she'd require as both countess and wife to the head PORF.

Needing to break the intangible pull of Bronwyn's attention, Landon pushed off from the desk and strode over to the seat facing her. This woman challenged him in ways no other had. His brain normally overruled his physical desires without resistance. Mayhap Bronwyn's intellectual appeal was the cause for his inability to control his bodily attraction to her. Hastily grabbing his coat and hat from the seat, he sat down and laid them over his lap to hide her obvious effect upon him. Landon adjusted his posture one last time and resumed observing the woman he hoped would accept his offer of marriage.

Her stare never faltered. The woman had worked alongside him for years. She was fully aware of his faults and weaknesses, especially his inability to back down from a challenge. The silence had become a test of wills. Who would give in and be the first to speak?

His brow creased as he struggled to recall a time when Bronwyn had ever conceded the argument during a debate or been the first to relent. Previously as lead barrister of the firm, Landon's primary purpose was to represent clients. He had left the running of the office to his brother, who doggedly employed the best person suited for the position regardless of their sex or background, resulting in the Neale & Sons staff being a mixed bag of individuals. In the case of hiring Landon's personal secretary, Christopher unconventionally hired a woman —Bronwyn.

He missed having a set routine. Pouring over case files, representing his clients in court, but most of all, debating with Bronwyn at length. She wasn't intimidated by him and never complained of the hours he required her to spend at the firm. Landon's shoulders rolled slightly forward. *Damnation.* He had been a self-absorbed taskmaster. A quick self-assessment and Landon let out a low groan. His propensity to demand excellence had not diminished. If anything, after becoming an earl and head PORF, they had intensified.

Bronwyn's lips curved into a smirk, in effect declaring herself the winner as he had been the first to emit a sound.

She leaned forward. "How may I be of assistance to you, Lord Hadfield?"

He may have lost this round, but he wasn't about to lose the next. "Tell me your surname."

"Why?"

Since the day he recovered the rondure, deeming him head PORF, over six months ago, not a soul had dared to

8

challenge him. With the exception of Theo and now the woman staring back at him.

Landon swallowed a groan returning his focus to the task at hand. "How else will I know who to ask for permission to marry you?"

Bronwyn jumped up from her seat. "Marry me?" A frown appeared on her features. She took a deep breath, and the deep creases in her brow disappeared. Leaning down, Bronwyn planted her palms on top of the desk. "I beg your pardon, Lord Hadfield. Are you attempting to propose?"

It was not the reaction Landon had hoped for. But her position over the table afforded him a lovely view of her chest, which mollified his agitation at her outburst and mocking tone. He shouldn't be vexed. Her lack of fear and ability to take him to task were the reasons Landon wanted Bronwyn for his countess.

He tugged on his cravat and blundered on. "Yes, I wish for us to be wed by week's end." He had the special license. All he needed was her agreement.

Her eyes roamed over his features. She cocked her head inquisitively. "Lord Hadfield, are you unwell?"

"No. Why would you suggest I was?"

"Your cheeks are flushed, and you suggested the mad notion that you wish for us to wed."

"It's not an insane idea."

Bronwyn rounded the desk to stand before him. She pressed the back of her hand to his forehead and then quickly removed it. "Well, you don't have a fever."

His skin might be cool to the touch, but his blood was

a-boil after the barest graze of her hand. Wedging a finger under his cravat, he tugged hard. He'd roast like a pig if she were to trail her palms over his naked body.

She waved a hand in front of his face. Head cocked to one side, Bronwyn asked, "Did you experience a head injury recently? It might explain your absurd proposal."

Perhaps from Bronwyn's point of view, his unexpected reappearance and bungled opening statements would give her cause to question his well-being. "I can assure you I'm quite well. There is nothing wrong with my head nor my wish to wed...you."

She placed her hands on her hips. "We haven't spoken in over twenty-four months."

It had actually been seven hundred and forty-one days. He had counted every single one since he last laid eyes on her.

Bronwyn drummed her fingers at her side. "You know nothing about me. Not even my surname." She dropped her gaze to his chest. "I'm no fresh-faced lady looking for a husband, especially not to a titled gentleman such as yourself. I'm not even from a wealthy merchant family, and I'm not..."

Landon placed a finger over her soft lips. The touch was meant to simply silence her, but as soon as he came into contact with her smooth skin, his brain misfired, sending heated waves of desire through him.

Landon blurted, "Your surname. I'll not ask again." Desperation was causing him to behave like a boor, instead of executing his oft-practiced pleas for Bronwyn to marry him. He would apologize and attempt to persuade her with the arguments he'd originally crafted.

When Bronwyn pursed her lips against his finger, he flinched and withdrew. The daring minx jutted her chin up, boldly staring into his eyes. Relieved to know she hadn't changed in the past months, he waited for her answer.

Seconds ticked by. He was determined not to give in and lose the battle. He loved her spirited nature, but he wouldn't always be able to accede to her demands.

Rolling her eyes, she answered, "Cadby."

The name sparked an alarm in his mind. He shook his head, dropped to one knee, and pried her small hand from her hip. His hand engulfed hers. "Miss Bronwyn Cadby, will you do me the great honor of marrying me?"

"Are you asking, or are you merely phrasing a command in the form of a question?"

Of course, the woman wouldn't simply say yes and jump for joy. Most women would cheer at the prospect of becoming a countess. Not her. She had to scrutinize his intentions.

"Very well, I shall address each of your concerns." Rising to his feet, Landon continued, "While we have not been in contact for years, I confess you have been at the forefront of my mind every day since we last spoke."

The corner of Bronwyn's lips twisted as if she didn't believe him.

Squeezing her hand, he continued, "I know everything I need to know about you. I'm not a fortune hunter in need of funds. However, I am in need of a wife and heir. You are the woman I want."

The crease between Bronwyn's eyebrows deepened. His ability to formulate highly persuasive arguments had failed, for the woman clearly remained unconvinced.

Landon squared his shoulders and added, "It's not a titled lady I'm seeking. I can assure you there is no other woman of my acquaintance who will fulfill the position as adeptly as you. I choose you to be the next Countess of Hadfield. Do you accept?" When she remained silent, Landon added, "It's a query, not a demand."

"Then you will allow me a day to consider." Her lips twitched as if she was resisting a smile. It was enough to convince Landon she would ultimately agree to marry him.

He rolled to his full height. "I'll return tomorrow for your answer." The alarm bells had yet to cease in his mind, and he would be a fool to ignore his intuition, which had proven to be his savior since inheriting the Hadfield title.

He turned to leave, but curiosity about what the woman would feel like in his arms got the better of him. Landon swiveled and came face to face with a bewildered Bronwyn. His arm wrapped about her waist as she swayed. Although she wasn't the swooning type, her faltering meant she wasn't entirely unaffected by his closeness.

Leaning in, Landon whispered into her ear, "Until tomorrow."

Reluctantly he released his hold as she twisted to

return to her seat behind what once was his papa's desk. She grabbed a file from the top of a stack and opened it with a flourish.

With a slight hop in his step, he left her to work. Yes, Bronwyn was exactly the woman he needed as a wife.

CHAPTER TWO

The black marks on the parchment before Bronwyn blurred. Her mind was a mass of confusion. Landon Neale, Lord Hadfield, Head PORF and the man who crept into her dreams nightly, had proposed—to her! He claimed she had invaded his daily thoughts, exactly as he occupied hers. How was that possible? His admission set her heart to racing, but from panic or joy, she wasn't sure which.

Snapping the file in front of her closed, she placed the folder upon a pile and then moved it a second time to its original stack. Mr. Neale had requested full summaries by the morn, but after Lord Hadfield's proposal, how was she to focus?

During the six years she'd been in the man's employ, he never once inquired about her family. She questioned whether or not he was even aware of her position within the Network. Even when she had disclosed her surname, he hadn't seemed to make the connection.

Eight years ago, Bronwyn had vied for the position of Landon's secretary to keep her true purpose—protecting him—secret. That was when he remained unmarked and unaware of his family's ties to the Crown. Her dad and Lady Theo's papa, the Earl of Hadfield at the time, had argued it was too dangerous for her. The likelihood of her obtaining the position of personal secretary was slim, given it was a position typically reserved for men. But after a few persuasive arguments, they relented and allowed her to apply for the post. Thankfully, Landon was due in court on the day of the interviews, and Mr. Christopher Neale had conducted them and hired for the position. Mr. Neale was two years Landon's junior and, while an extremely talented debater, was no match for Bronwyn. Never had an hour gone by with such speed, and every week since, her meetings with Mr. Neale provided Bronwyn with an opportunity to exercise her mind and broaden her knowledge.

Mr. Neale barreled into her office with his usual flare of exuberance. "Right, Miss Bronwyn, I've prepared an excellent critique of the Coleman case. You won't be able to..." He stopped short and turned to look behind him. "Whatever is the matter?"

The two brothers couldn't be more opposite in disposition despite their strong physical resemblance. Landon was a fiercely independent leader and thrived on hard work, while Mr. Neale tended to rule by consensus and employed a laissez-faire attitude to life.

Mr. Neale advanced a step. "Are you well?"

"Have you spoken to Lord Hadfield?"

"I didn't cheat by seeking out Landon's help. I formulated my arguments all on my own, thank you very much."

"That's not what I meant. Your brother was here earlier; did he not seek you out?"

"Landon was here?" Mr. Neale chuckled. "I imagine he was quite surprised to find his office reassigned."

"Your brother did seem rather nonplussed by the fact."

Mr. Neale's gaze intensified. "Hmm. What did he want?"

"You don't know?"

"I'm not the one practicing to be on the witness stand in this instance. Now, tell me why Landon was here." He stood and placed his right hand behind his back and the left on his hip. It was the stance he always took when he was about to begin cross-examination.

Bronwyn stared at Mr. Neale, the sole reason she was allowed by the Network to remain employed at the law offices after Landon's departure. Abiding by Landon's orders, her dad had yet to place the mark upon Mr. Neale's body that would indicate the man was indeed a PORF. Her duty was to ensure no harm came to Mr. Neale. How was she to answer her employer? If Mr. Neale bore the mark, she would have had no choice but to obey and disclose Landon's purpose. Since Mr. Neale didn't, and Landon hadn't sought out his brother's time, she was at a loss for the appropriate response. Bronwyn rolled back her shoulders and replied, "I'm not at liberty to say."

"Was he here to reclaim his office?"

"No." Bronwyn's knee bounced up and down under the desk. She reached out and adjusted each of the piles of files in front of her to keep her hands occupied.

"Did he inquire as to my whereabouts?"

"No." If it had been Landon standing before her, he'd simply demand an answer or stare her down as he had earlier. Instead, Mr. Neale would doggedly ask questions until she relented, or he'd muddle through the facts based on her answers and figure it all out on his own.

"Did he receive what he came for?"

Bronwyn hesitated. "No."

Blast!

Mr. Neale's eyebrows rose at her answer. Pauses of any sort were a telltale sign of weakness or uncertainty. To a barrister, it meant they should further ponder and continue the line of questioning. Her employer turned, placing his back to her and murmured to himself—

"Not office related.

"He hinted at having made a decision, yet he's not shown a preference for any of the ladies on Theo's list.

"He was rather prickly this morn.

"Aha. By Jove, Landon's finally come to his senses and figured it out."

Mr. Neale was too clever by half. When he rounded to face her again, his features had softened, no longer accusatory. "My brother was here to see *you* and to pose a specific question. Did you say yes?"

She reached up and withdrew the pencil from her

hair, setting her bun askew. "I requested a day to consider his proposal."

Christopher came to stand next to her. "You can say no if you want to." His knees cracked as he crouched down beside her. "I'll speak to him if you would like."

"In my position, *No* is not an option."

"Of course, it is! Landon would never force you to marry him."

"You don't understand."

"No, it is not I who is mistaken, it is you. I may pretend to be oblivious to the workings of the Network and my family dealings, but I'm fully aware of who and what my brother is. I also know that he would never order or command you to marry him. So, what is your answer to be?"

"That's the issue—I don't know what the right answer is."

He gave her his brotherly look. "Very well, let's reason it out together, shall we?"

Bronwyn nodded. She had always considered Mr. Neale rather like an older brother. If she married Landon, he would, in fact, be that.

Mr. Neale rose and paced in front of her desk. "Landon is not one to make decisions rashly. He must have given this much thought."

"Yes, but why me? Never once, in the six years we worked together, did he ever act anything but the gentleman. Why not offer for a young lady of the ton?"

Mr. Neale lips twisted into a smirk. "Now, you know what I'm about to say. *Never make assumptions until you have all the facts*. Have you met these young ladies you speak of?"

"No. However, I am kept rather well informed. Especially of your cousin Lady Theo."

"Theo is not young and definitely not representative of the ladies I've been subjected to meeting these two years past."

"In any case, Lord Hadfield should marry a lady, not someone like me." Bronwyn stopped herself from declaring that countesses are supposed to be refined, well mannered; not brazen, and outspoken.

"I don't follow. Explain your reasoning."

"He needs a gently bred wife to host parties and balls, not a shopkeeper's daughter."

"Then your exceptional communication and organizational skills will come in handy."

Communication skills, ha! It had taken hours, days, and weeks of practice to eliminate all traces of her cockney accent and colloquialisms from her speech. Bronwyn suspected her abilities with a dagger, and legal knowledge would be of little interest to the ladies of the ton. Those ladies would be unlike the women within the Network, who were always eager to learn self-protection and ways to keep their men out of trouble.

Bronwyn shrugged. "Mr. Neale, you are not helping and are clearly mistaken."

"Am I not? In fact, after considering the matter, I fully comprehend Landon's reasoning for selecting you as the next Countess of Hadfield. Also, you shall have to start addressing me as Christopher and not thinking of me as Mr. Neale." He grinned, winking at her—her future brother-in-law was a rogue at heart, exactly like his brother.

"I am curious how you came to such a conclusion," Bronwyn said. "Care to share your wisdom?"

"You shall have to figure it out on your own. I'm confident it won't take you long." With one hand on the door handle, Christopher turned to say, "Might I suggest you pay a visit to your friend Ms. Lennox."

"How do you know of Emma?"

"While I've not had the pleasure of meeting the woman, Theo speaks rather highly of her."

"Mr. Neale..." At the man's scowl, Bronwyn corrected herself. "Christopher, you are a genius. Emma will know exactly how to handle the situation."

"And you can advise her on your trousseau." Christopher left and closed the door before she could respond.

The mountain of files on her desk would take hours to complete.

The latch of the door clicked and she jumped as Christopher popped his head back in. "The reports can wait. Landon will not." Her employer disappeared as quickly as he had reappeared.

Sliding her chair back to stand, Bronwyn was hit by a thought—*life from this day forward will never be the same.*

THE WIND PICKED UP, sending Emma's store sign swinging forward and back. Bronwyn peered up at the harped angel, a symbol of seniority amongst those in the Network, and smiled as it glittered against the sunlight. Her best friend's family had served PORFs for generations, as her own had.

What would her parents say when she returned home?

Her dad remained skeptical of Landon's worth, despite him being the holder of the rondure. Bronwyn grinned as she recalled her dad's grumblings the night Lord Archbroke had brought Landon to their home to receive the mark.

A small hand wrapped about Bronwyn's arm and tugged her toward the door. "Lawd above. Why are ye loiterin' on me stoop?" Emma asked.

"I was..."

Emma shut the door behind them and turned the sign over to indicate her store was closed for the day. "Well, how long do I have?"

She shouldn't be surprised Emma had already learned the news. Word traveled at precipitous speed within the Network. "When did you find out?"

"About an hour ago." Emma bustled about moving bolts of fabric. "Lady Theo sent over a missive I found intriguin'."

"What did it say?"

"Somethin' about ye bein' the reason her *nap*"—Emma wiggled her brows at Bronwyn—"was cut short or somethin' or other."

"*Emma!*"

Her best friend stilled and scowled. "Don't get all in a

huff. Lady Theo said in her note she'd support ye no matter yer decision. I, on the other hand, will only support the bleedin' correct decision."

"And that would be?"

Emma grabbed her upper arms. "Bronwyn Cadby, stop bein' a goose." Releasing Bronwyn, Emma grabbed a swath of silk. "I'm goin' to create ye the most stunnin' bridal gown and fill yer trousseau with dresses that all the ladies of the ton will envy."

Bronwyn glanced at the divine pink silk held in her best friend's hand. She wanted to scream *Lord Hadfield should be marrying a lady*. Instead, she glared at Emma and said, "I'm not a lady. Countesses are ladies."

Lifting the fabric up to Bronwyn's cheek, Emma said, "Ye are a woman worthy of becomin' Countess Hadfield. Plus, it was his choice to make, and Lord Hadfield chose ye."

"Don't you find that odd?"

"No. Ye're beautiful, smart, trustworthy, and loyal." Emma pulled her arm away and turned to assess the material she had amassed before them. "*And,* none of those hoytie toytie ladies have any of the skills a wife to the Head PORF needs."

"What qualities do you suppose I possess that they do not?"

Emma placed both hands on her hips as she swirled about. "Well..."

"See. You can't."

"Give me a moment! Not everyone can rattle off arguments as fast as ye."

"He doesn't even know I'm part of the Network!"

"Blimey! All these years and ye never let it slip. Ye're the bloomin' master of disguise. See, ye proved it. There is not another woman better suited than ye to be his wife." Emma giggled then added, "Ye know I'm right."

Bronwyn released a sigh and flopped down upon the chaise. "If I accept, I'd be placing my family and closest friends in grave danger."

"All right." Emma threw her hands up and then slapped them against her thighs. "Ye're right. Ye should say no. Happy now?"

"Hmm..." Bronwyn draped her arm over her eyes.

"Wot is wrong with ye? I thought ye'd seize the bleedin' opportunity to rule over me."

"That would be one advantage. But..."

Bronwyn abruptly sat up, hitting Emma's forehead. Simultaneously, they said, "Oww."

Emma reached for Bronwyn's hand. "Is it Lord Hadfield?"

"Not exactly. Besides being aware of how Landon takes his tea and coffee, and that he is a brilliant barrister, what do I really know of him?"

"Lor! Wot do ye need to know?" Dreamy-eyed, Emma tilted her head. "He's kind, a bleedin' excellent leader, and oh, those *dimples*!"

"Why don't you marry him then?"

"I would've if he had asked *me*. But marriage ain't for me." Emma released Bronwyn's hand and stood by the table of buttons and ribbons.

"That is utter rubbish. You simply haven't met a man

worthy of your love." She walked over and gave her best friend a brief hug. Emma was the eldest child and had always placed her family's welfare before her own. Opening up the modiste shop had meant working many hours and left little time for courting.

Emma grabbed a handful of buttons and let them filter through her fingers. "I don't understand yer hesitation."

"He's titled. There will be social engagements, balls, dinners, and such." Bronwyn ran a finger over a wide emerald green ribbon.

"Lady Theo will not let ye fail."

Bronwyn added, "We know nothing of each other."

"Ye worked for the man for years, and not once did ye ever utter a complaint about him. Ye will have the rest of yer lives to learn each other's preferences and habits."

"When did you master the art of counter-arguments?"

"I learned from the bloomin' best." Emma wrapped Bronwyn in a hug. "I need at least another week."

Bronwyn returned the hug. "A week? You have two days."

Emma groaned and said, "Oh, ye're goin' be a tyrant."

CHAPTER THREE

*T*he tinkle of the bell above her head announced Bronwyn's arrival at her dad's store. Her nose crinkled at the scent of dried, slightly moldy tobacco leaves. Working in the Neales' law offices, where snuff and cigars were frowned upon, had given her a respite from the pungent smell.

Harold, her brother, glanced up from a perfectly balanced scale. "Watcha doin' walking in through the front?"

Bronwyn turned to face the door. Blimey, what was she thinking? Lost in practicing the speech she was to deliver to her parents, she had waltzed right into the store through the street entrance instead of the back door used by Network members and family.

Anxious to be done with the deed of informing her parents of Landon's preposterous idea to marry, she ignored her brother and walked through the store to the back. She raised a hand to push back the curtain to enter the small room where her dad kept the store's records, when Harold yelled, "He's upstairs."

Bronwyn froze. Upstairs held her dad's private office, where he conducted official Network affairs. Blood drained from her face. Had her dad already heard? With a fortifying breath, she marched around crates and boxes to the staircase that led up to her dad's office.

Skipping over the fifth step that creaked, Bronwyn crept her way up. On the landing, she paused and took inventory. Chin up. Straight back. Shoulders squared. Ready. Confronting her dad with the news was far worse than facing the guillotine.

As she neared the door, a familiar male voice boomed through the walls. "It's been near on six months since his return from the Continent. He can't continue to dally. He needs a bloody heir." Mr. Rutherford, a Network elder, was clearly agitated. She had no illusions about which *he* Rutherford was referring to—Landon. She crept closer to the door.

"Lady Archbroke suspects he's already decided upon someone." Her dad's sigh matched Rutherford's frustrated tone. "Our Lady Theo promises to alert us as soon as she can."

"But we need time to install the right staff to ensure the lady is worthy of holding such a position amongst us, and that is merely the preliminary work to be done."

Her stomach clenched. Everyone was expecting Landon to propose to a lady. She didn't know the first thing about being the wife of a titled gentleman, let alone a PORF.

"I'm fully aware of what has to be done. There is still time. Lord Hadfield will have to properly court the lady, which will allow us to have everything in place before the wedding." Her dad's voice faded and strengthened as he spoke. He must be pacing. He never paced unless he was upset.

"Bronwyn Cadby!" Her mum's harsh whisper scared her straight.

Swiveling to face her mum, Bronwyn murmured, "I was..."

"I know exactly what ye were doin'. I raised ye to know better."

Bronwyn bowed her head and replied, "Yes, Mum."

"Harold came and got me. Said ye were behavin' strange." Her mum pressed the back of her hand to Bronwyn's forehead. "Ye're not sick, are ye?"

"No, Mum. But I must speak with Dad." Bronwyn held her breath as she waited.

Stepping around Bronwyn, her mum rapped on the door.

"Enter."

Following close on her mum's heels, like she had as a child when summoned by her dad, Bronwyn marched resolutely in her mum's shadow.

"Rutherford, please excuse the interruption, but I must speak with my husband." When Rutherford remained seated, her mum added, "Alone."

Rutherford stood and donned his hat and coat. "Think upon it, Cadby. I'll be eagerly awaiting your call to convene." He tipped his hat as he passed them to leave.

As soon as the latch fell into place, her mum tugged Bronwyn to her side. "Well, git on with it. Speak."

Her dad turned from the window, and his knowing gaze fell upon her. He couldn't possibly know what news she bore, yet he always seemed to anticipate what she was about to say. Wringing her hands behind her, Bronwyn said, "Lord Hadfield paid me a visit today."

Neither parent responded. Their features completely blank as they waited for her to continue. The speech Bronwyn had prepared deserted her mind. Instead, she blurted, "His lordship has asked me to marry him." As she expected, her mum gave her a broad smile, and her dad's features darkened with a fierce scowl.

Her dad stomped over to his chair behind the desk and sat. "He's already procured the special license. You will wed as soon as I give him my blessing." He picked up a news sheet and read.

She was not the fainting type, but a lack of air and the twinkling stars before her eyes had Bronwyn clutching the edge of the desk and inhaling deeply. She'd predicted her dad wouldn't deny a request by a PORF, but she hadn't even managed to share her plan, and her dad was already done with the topic.

Her mum rubbed soothing circles upon her back. "All will be well. No time to dawdle; we must get you ready."

No. Landon was to marry a lady, not her. Of all people, her parents should know this. Taking in a deep breath, Bronwyn straightened and faced her mum. "Lord Hadfield is making a mistake by offering for me. It is a tradition that a PORF marry one of their own."

The snap of the paper being straightened brought her focus back to her dad. "He is risking too much! He'll expose the Network if he marries me. Marrying a commoner will raise suspicions. Consider the possibility of all our secrets being exposed if someone takes an interest and digs into my background. It's not how things work. He'll disrupt the balance."

She heaved in another breath, but before Bronwyn could continue, her dad said, "I'll not hear another word. You will marry Lord Hadfield."

Fustian!

If her dad would not hear her pleas, she'd wait until she had her mum alone. She let her mum guide her from her dad's office. As soon as they'd walked down the hall to the connecting door that led to the family's living quarters, Bronwyn placed a hand on her mum's arm. "You have to make Dad understand."

Her mum led her into the kitchen and placed a kettle in the fire.

Bronwyn needed her mum to comprehend her plight. Her mum was her last hope, the only person capable of convincing her dad to put a stop to this madness. "I'm not the right woman for Lord Hadfield. I'll bring shame upon him. I've no idea how to behave like a lady. He needs someone who can host balls and house parties, run multiple households, and forge alliances amongst the ladies of the ton." Bronwyn paused and went to the cabinet to get the teacups. "I know naught of those things, and I've nothing in common with the duchesses, marchionesses, and countesses his wife would need to befriend in order to assist with PORF affairs." She plopped down on the bench as her mum calmly reached for a cloth, and then the boiling kettle.

Pouring steaming water into the well worn tea pot, her mum said, "Lord Hadfield has had the special license in his possession for over a month now. As head PORF, his actions and directives have been rather...deliberate. I'm sure he gave the decision to marry and to whom much thought." She set the kettle down. Placing her warm hand beneath Bronwyn's chin, her mum tilted Bronwyn's head up and met her eyes. "He was wise to choose you."

Bronwyn poured the barely steeped tea into their cups. Her mum sipped tea, eyeing her with one eyebrow cocked. It was as if her mum was challenging her to find a counter-argument. But her mind had wandered after the revelation that Landon had held on to the special license for a month.

Bronwyn tapped her finger against her teacup as she contemplated a plan that would allow them both time to be sure marriage was the best solution.

Her mum stood up, winked, and took Bronwyn's cup from her hands. "Child, you are smart and brave. I'm extremely proud of you, and I know you will not shame our family."

Whatever plan she devised, she'd ensure it would not end in disgrace.

CHAPTER FOUR

*T*wisted between his bed linens, Landon groaned as the image of the three piles of case-work sitting atop Bronwyn's desk reappeared—haunting him as he attempted to sleep. Rolling out of bed, Landon hastily donned his shirt and breeches without the assistance of a valet, as he had done many a time before he inherited the earldom.

Landon grinned as he tiptoed through the hall and down the stairs of his townhouse. It was like he was twenty-two again, leaving his bachelor lodgings in the middle of the night to get a head start on the day's work to prove to his papa that he would be capable of running the firm one day. A surge of excitement at the prospect of utilizing his legal training had his feet pounding against the pavement.

Out of breath, Landon stood frozen at the front door of the Neale & Sons offices. He stared down at his shadow and asked, "What are you afraid of?" The answer was complicated and not completely formulated in his mind. Landon shook his head and entered the quiet building.

In the peaceful dark, Landon sat at his old desk, a stalwart reminder of his previous path in his papa's footsteps. But would he face the same untimely demise as his papa, due to their shared lung condition? Landon might not be on this earth much longer. Christopher would be miserable as earl, and that was but a portion of the responsibilities he'd leave to his unsuspecting brother. His little brother would also inherit the rondure, which brought about danger and a slew of obligations that Landon himself was trying to unravel. He needed an heir and a wife who was intelligent and courageous enough to guide his son should he die early. He needed Bronwyn. With a frown, he pulled the first pile of files in front of him. *Deal with one matter at a time.*

SUNLIGHT FELL UPON THE DESK. Quill poised midair, Landon reviewed the summary before him. A swell of pride gained momentum and eased the tension in his chest. Breathing easier than he had in months, Landon grinned at the tall stack of files at the corner of Bronwyn's desk.

His brother's voice wafted through the office. Landon pulled out his pocket watch; it was later in the morning than he had realized. He chuckled as Christopher's cheery greetings to the staff became louder and louder. He missed working alongside his brother every day.

The door swung open, and Christopher popped his head in. "What the devil are you doing here?" Christopher sauntered into Bronwyn's office and slid into the client chair across the desk.

Landon ran a hand over his jaw covered in stubble. "I merely sought to help prepare a few summaries."

"Don't you have more pressing issues to deal with?"

"Not at this time." He rolled his head from side to side. His neck and shoulder muscles were no longer accustomed to being strained for extended periods. In recent months, the only burden Landon had carried was the pressure of selecting a wife. Bronwyn's sweet features flashed before his mind's eye.

"Really?" Christopher sat back in his chair and crossed his legs. "Have you practiced your closing arguments?"

Whether it was from a lack of sleep or his distracted thoughts, Landon stumbled over his brother's logic. "Beg pardon?"

"Perhaps you should run them by me before she arrives."

She? Christopher gave him a wide grin. His brother must have heard of his failed proposal. Likely he'd overheard the staff at the townhouse discussing it this morning. Landon had made the mistake of visiting Theo after his meeting with Bronwyn. The walls of her townhouse were paper thin. Theo was the only woman whose discretion and judgment he trusted. He desperately needed her insight into why Bronwyn had not immediately accepted his offer of marriage, and he sought her advice on to how to rectify the situation. Instead of providing the guidance he wished for, Theo had simply told him not to act like an ignoramus and then applauded his choice of wife. Landon realized the error of his visit as he walked through the foyer to leave and received full, approving smiles from the household staff. The Network was abuzz with his decision to wed.

Landon steepled his fingers. "Very well. Let's practice. I thought to start with: 'I apologize for not having adequately addressed your concerns...'" He paused at the thump of Christopher's hand landed on the desk.

"By Jove, no wonder Bronwyn requested a reprieve. You have absolutely no..."

Landon abruptly stood. "Since when did the two of you drop all pretense of formality?" Christopher's casual use of Bronwyn's Christian name inflamed Landon's guilt at his prolonged absence and neglect of Bronwyn and the firm.

Christopher rose to his full height, a mere inch shorter than Landon. "Are you daft? How else do you expect me to refer to my sister-to-be?"

"How presumptuous of you, since she has yet to agree to marry me."

His brother mumbled, "And they say he's the smart one." Christopher's smile faded. "*Bronwyn* has been infatuated with *you* from her very first day here at the office. I've wondered how long it would take you to come to your senses and make her an offer."

"Since day one?" Landon glared at his brother. "The woman has never batted her eyes at me, nor has she ever giggled at one of my jests."

Christopher rolled his eyes.

Landon wanted to slap himself on the head. He was a buffoon. "Do you think I've made a huge error?"

"In delaying your decision to wed? No. You inherited a mountain of debt and responsibilities along with a title that most would have turned and run from." Christopher tapped the desk. "Your biggest blunder yesterday was failing to express your true feelings for her. I suggest you rectify the situation today."

"That is my intention. If I succeed, I anticipate I'll be out of town for a spell. In my absence, you will have to escort Mama to balls, soirees, and such."

Christopher's shoulders sagged. "You know how much I detest being thrust amongst the ton."

"Our mother gains a wealth of information from these gatherings." Landon softened at his younger brother's obvious discomfort. "Name your price."

"What did Mama extract from you?"

"A promise to wed and beget an heir as soon as possible."

Laughter lit up Christopher's eyes. "A crate of brandy will be sufficient for me."

With a chuckle, Landon nodded, but his focus was on the door, which had swung open.

Bronwyn stepped into the office and paused at the sight of the two strikingly handsome brothers smiling at each other. Her attention, as always, was inexplicably drawn to the taller, older brother. Out of practice at masking her reactions to Landon, the tips of her ears and cheeks burned, and her pulse raced at the sight of his devilish dimple.

She swallowed and found her voice. "Gentlemen, am I interrupting?"

Christopher was the first to react. "No, I was on my way out." He moved to stand before her, then leaned in to whisper, "Take it easy on him. I've always wished for a sister like you."

Her cheeks were aflame. She bowed her head and said, "Didn't your mama tell you to be careful about what you wish for?"

With a chuckle, Christopher left the room, leaving her all alone with the man her entire family had sworn to obey and protect. Lifting her chin, she walked toward her desk, but Lord Hadfield stood in front of her chair. This was her office, no longer his. He should make way for her, but the man showed no inclination to make the gentlemanly gesture. Eyebrows angled down into a frown, she walked right up to Landon. "Excuse me."

She was mere inches away before he relented, bowing, and pulled the chair out further for her. Keeping her back to him, Bronwyn slipped into the chair and scooted it forward. She reached for one of the three pencils neatly arranged on the desktop. His warm breath grazed her neck as she swept up the loose tendrils of hair that had escaped her haphazard bun and stuck the pencil through her locks to hold them in place.

"I took the liberty of preparing the summaries for you."

She grabbed the folder from the top of the pile and opened it. "My thanks, but unnecessary."

Landon leaned in, looking over his work. "I hope they meet your expectations."

Ha! It was he who taught her how to examine the details and sift the minutiae from the facts. Her eyes fluttered closed, mimicking the sensations in her stomach. He was too close. She wouldn't be able to concentrate when her body screamed at her to lean into his. She snapped the file shut. "Everything appears to be in order. Mr. Neale will be pleased."

"Are *you* pleased?"

"Lord Hadfield..."

"I'd be honored if you would address me by my given name."

"Only in the event I agree to your proposal."

"What is preventing you from saying yes?"

Bronwyn reached into her hidden dress pocket and retrieved a carefully crafted list of queries. His answers wouldn't sway her response, but Landon's reactions would provide her with some insight into what the future might hold.

She held out the parchment for Landon.

His gaze shifted between the note and her eyes. "A list of demands?"

She withdrew the list and clutched it to her chest. "No, not demands. How mercenary."

Landon's dimple appeared. "A list of inquires then?" He tilted his head and placed his palm out.

"Yes." Instead of giving him the parchment, she replaced it in her pocket. "Three simple questions."

Landon straightened, and instead of taking the seat opposite her, he perched on the edge of the desk and placed one booted foot behind his calf. "Very well, let's begin."

"What has prompted your decision to wed?"

"My papa left this earth an early age from a lung condition that I too suffer from. It is imperative I sire an heir before I depart this world." His hazel eyes lacked their usual intensity. "The London air has progressively worsened over recent years, and the poor air quality has accelerated my condition."

In her skirt pocket, her hand balled into a fist as an ache settled in the center of her chest. The pain wasn't from the lack of romanticism; she hadn't expected Landon to profess undying love for her, but she was unprepared for the rawness of his voice as he shared his fears. "Why not remain in the country?"

He dipped his chin to his chest and tilted his head toward her. "You *know* that is not possible."

Yes, as earl he'd be expected at the House of Lords, and his dealings as Head PORF would need to be coordinated from London. With the right woman as a wife, he'd have another to share those burdens. Emma and her mum both assured her she possessed the skills Landon required of his countess. Bronwyn had never shunned a responsibility in her life, but the magnitude of having other people's lives in her hands weighed heavily on her heart and mind.

She squared her shoulders with false bravado. "Second question: How can you be certain we are suitably matched?"

"To clarify, that's your third inquiry. And the answer is—I can't be sure. You were right yesterday in pointing out that we are not well-acquainted despite having worked together for six years. However, I am acutely aware that I missed you these past two years." Landon leaned closer, resting his forearm over his thigh. "I apologize for being slow and not seeking you out sooner."

Bronwyn's heart stilled at the intensity in Landon's voice. His sincere apology left her short of breath. He hadn't been slow. Christopher had the right of it yesterday. Landon never made decisions in haste. Yet, Bronwyn couldn't fathom why he wanted *her* to be his wife. "I still have one last item to ask you. Do you know who my dad is?"

Landon chuckled. "I do indeed. Theo aided my memory and informed me he is the miserable old man who saw to it that I received the mark."

Bronwyn giggled. Her dad was a bit of a geezer. "Yes, for generations, it has been our family's honor to bestow the mark upon PORFs. Then you understand that I've sworn an oath and it's impossible for me to say no."

He brushed a finger along the side of her face, and as his finger came to rest under her chin, he tilted her face up. Gazes locked. Landon said, "We will not wed unless it is what you desire."

The way the word desire rolled off his tongue sent sparks up her spine. He leaned back, resting his hand upon his knee. Keenly aware he was giving her space to decide, Bronwyn rubbed the back of her neck where the sparks ended.

Breathless, she concentrated on the point she was attempting to convey. "It matters not what my wishes are. I'll not dishonor my family by denying you."

"Your wishes matter to me." He grinned, displaying his heart-melting dimple. "But before you give me your final answer, I too have a series of queries for you. First, do you find me unattractive?"

Landon was far from ugly. Like Emma, Bronwyn's insides fluttered at the sight of his dimple, and while she might hate to admit it, she did appreciate his fine looks. "Not in the least."

"Do you trust me?"

"Absolutely." Bronwyn shared her dad's philosophy that trust must be earned, and Landon had long ago won her trust.

He focused on her lips. "I want to kiss you. Would you like that?"

She stared into his eyes. The sudden glimmer of mischief made her uneasy. It was almost as if he was teasing her. Bronwyn stood, the back of her knees pushing her chair back. With him perched on the desk, she didn't have to roll onto her tiptoes to place her hands upon his chest. Eyes closed, she lifted her chin, ready for him to kiss her.

Instead of his lips pressing against hers, warm fingers brushed against the side of Bronwyn's neck. Landon's palm cradled her jaw as the pad of his thumb ran along her bottom lip. Bronwyn's breath caught in her throat.

"Tell me you want to marry me first before I kiss you." His thumb glided over her lip a second time.

Blinking her eyes open, she swallowed. "Yes."

Leaning closer, Landon whispered in her ear, "I want to hear you say it."

"I'll marry you."

His lips swept along her exposed neck down to her shoulder. Seeking to stabilize herself, she curled her hands, bunching the material of his waistcoat. She couldn't decide if she wanted to pull him closer or push him away. That dilemma fled her mind as his tongue followed the ridge of her collar bone. Landon peppered light kisses upon the swell of her bosom, causing her breathing to hasten.

Landon was renowned for his self-control and restraint. His leisurely exploration was either a testament to his willpower or his roguish nature attempting to torture her.

No longer willing to wait, Bronwyn cupped Landon's face and brought his mouth to meet her own. Soft but firm lips molded to hers. An urge to taste him had Bronwyn parting her lips, allowing his tongue to seek out hers. A burst of exhilaration roared through her veins. She wanted more. Wrapping her arms about his neck, she threaded her hand through his hair and pressed him closer. Boys had tried to kiss her before, cornering her and crushing their mouths in brutal, crude attacks. This was nothing of the kind. Landon was no boy, and she was apparently skilled in the art of kissing.

Landon pulled back. For a moment, she didn't want the spell to end. Soft kisses upon her eyelids prompted her to open her eyes. His dimple greeted her. She had agreed to marry Landon.

When her pulse returned to normal, she reached into her skirt pocket on the left that held another list.

"What is that?"

"My demands."

Landon laughed. "I knew you'd have a list of demands. Pray tell. What's on it?"

"First, I'll not wed in front of the ton at St. Georges. Second, Emma needs another day to have everything readied before we leave for Scotland. Third, you have to speak to my dad tonight."

"Let me make sure I understand. You don't want to wait the three weeks for the banns to be read, and you want to hie off to Gretna Green and be married over an anvil."

"I know you already procured a special license, so a delay of three weeks was never an option."

"Have you shared your demands with anyone? Has the Network already begun preparations?"

"Of course I've not shared my list with another. No one would think me daft enough to actually make requests of the head PORF."

"Grand. Then there is room for negotiation?"

"Absolutely not."

Landon gathered her up in his arms and whispered, "And that is exactly why you are the one for me."

Bronwyn smiled, but she still believed it implausible that she was really perfect for him.

CHAPTER FIVE

*T*he bell over Rutherford's door tinkled as Landon entered. He smiled, glad that Cadby had agreed to meet at Rutherford's jewelry store rather than at his tobacco shop. A shiver ran down Landon's spine at the memory of entering Cadby's store. It had taken Landon weeks to recover from his visit. Apart from the fact his skin needed to heal after Cadby had taken his leisure in tattooing the mark upon his hip, his lungs had ached after inhaling the tobacco fumes for hours.

Rutherford's gray head appeared. "Lord Hadfield, I wasn't expecting you for another thirty minutes." The old man rushed to the door and flipped the sign to indicate he was no longer open for business.

"I thought I might browse your selection of rings before we begin the evening's proceedings." Landon perused the glass cabinets. Bronwyn was exceedingly practical—what type of jewel would suit her best?

Rather than offering suggestions, Rutherford disappeared into the back.

Bronwyn was born in October. Running his finger along the edge of the counter, he tried to recall which stone represented her birth month.

"Might I suggest you select a ring from this collection?" The jeweler pushed forward a tray with three exquisite rings atop dark blue velvet.

Landon picked up the center ring, drawn to its unique design. "What is this stone called?" The pink jewels that surrounded the center stone reminded him of Bronwyn's lips and their kiss.

"It's an opal, my lord, surrounded by pink tourmaline. They are Miss Cadby's birthstones."

How fitting. Landon raised the ring to the dwindling rays of sunlight. "I'll take this one."

Rutherford held out his palm. "Very well, I shall make certain it is cleaned and polished and delivered to you in the morn."

"I'd prefer to take it with me when I leave after our meeting."

The man's white brows angled down. "Certainly." Rutherford snatched the ring from Landon's hand and walked toward the back again, mumbling. "And to think, we're about to lose Bronwyn to the likes of him. Tsk. Tsk."

Landon grinned at Rutherford's comment. It was fortunate he had fallen for a woman the Network held in such high regard. Wandering about the store, Landon examined the exquisite pieces of jewelry in the cabinets. A ruby and diamond choker caught his interest. Fantasizing the piece around Bronwyn's delicate throat, he jumped when a meaty hand landed on his shoulder.

Landon spun around to find his friend Gilbert Talbot, Earl of Waterford, standing next to him. Waterford's features were grim. "Cadby is not pleased. Why did you not seek him out prior to approaching his daughter?"

Crossing his arms across his chest, Landon replied, "If I'd known her surname prior to my proposal, I would have."

Waterford chuckled. "Apparently, some secrets are safe within the Network."

"What are you doing here?"

His friend's eyes widened, and his eyebrows slanted inward. One was arched higher than the other. Landon hadn't asked with the intention of provoking either reaction, but he had expected only the elders to be in attendance.

"I'm one of the six council members."

"You are one of the *elders*?"

"Don't look so surprised. The council is comprised of the eldest living member of the original six families that founded the Network. I'm the eldest of my line. Come. I'll introduce you to the remaining five members."

Curse Archbroke and his cursory review of the Network and its workings. Landon suspected it was due to Archbroke's own limited knowledge, not that the man intentionally withheld information. "Who of the PORFs are aware of which families make up this illustrious council?"

The crease between Waterford's brows deepened. "You will be the only PORF to know. While Network members vow to protect and assist PORFs, the PORFs do not govern our organization. The elders' council is our ruling body."

"Thank you for clarifying. I still have much to learn." Landon followed Waterford to the back.

Seated at a long table were three women of middling ages. Cadby and Rutherford stood as he entered the room. Waterford motioned for him to take the seat at the head of the table. The council members alternated male and female on each side of the table.

Waterford took the seat to Landon's right. "Lord Hadfield, allow me to introduce you to the Network elders." Waterford turned to his right. "Mrs. Lennox. Her daughter, Emma, is your cousin Theo's modiste." The woman dipped her head in Landon's direction and then promptly turned to her right as Waterford continued. "You already know Rutherford. Across from Rutherford is Mrs. Cornwell, whose family has served in the Marquess of Burke's household for generations."

Landon smiled, revealing his dimple. Instead of a blush rising to the woman's cheeks, which was the typical response from women of all ages when he displayed the small dent in his cheek, Mrs. Cornwell's lips thinned into a straight line. Landon inwardly groaned; he was in for a long night of discussions.

Waterford's gaze landed on Cadby. "The man next to

Mrs. Cornwell is Cadby, who you know is Bronwyn's papa. And last but not least is Mrs. Barnwell. She and her husband own a coaching inn, the Lone Dove. Mrs. Barnwell will be leading the proceedings this evening."

Thank goodness. The woman was the only one whose glare did not contain a hint of skepticism.

"Lord Hadfield, welcome." Mrs. Barnwell glanced at each guest in turn before returning to Landon. "It has come to our attention you have expressed an interest in our dear Bronwyn."

Landon cleared his suddenly dry throat. "Yes. I sent a request around to Mr. Cadby's establishment in the hopes I'd have the honor of his time and to seek out his blessing. However, Mr. Cadby informed me I was to apply to the council for permission to marry his daughter."

"There are many reasons why we are protective of our children. But in Bronwyn's case, we are ever more so, for she holds two important roles within our organization. She is next in line to represent the Cadby family on this council, and she is the sole representative of the next generation as voted by her peers." Mrs. Barnwell turned to Rutherford. "While we allow Lord Hadfield time to process all I have shared, Rutherford, will you please have the refreshments brought in?"

As Rutherford left the room, Cadby's features revealed nothing of his thoughts, only his displeasure. Landon attempted to school his shock and annoyance at his lack of knowledge. Marrying Bronwyn would disrupt the dynamics within the Network. But he needed her more than they did. His mind and body were attracted to no other woman. Not a single lady of the ton had managed to capture his interest for longer than a few minutes before his mind would flash an image of Bronwyn. Then all he could do was compare the lady to Bronwyn. None were as interesting or alluring.

Utilizing every ounce of restraint and willpower, Landon remained still with his spine and shoulders steeled straight, bearing the weight of every council member's regard. He ruminated over the progress of the meeting, while the council members continued their evaluation of him. Fears of inadequacy that needled him every day since he obtained the rondure crept to the forefront of his mind. A bitter taste flooded his mouth as he bit down on the inside corner of his lower lip.

Rutherford returned, leading a line of servants laden with food and drink, which confirmed Landon's suspicion: he would not be leaving any time soon. Landon glanced at Waterford from the corner of his eye. Until now, Waterford's demeanor had remained impartial, but there was a keenness in the man's eye as he assessed Landon's reactions. While Landon had spent months traveling with Waterford and considered him a close friend, he hadn't totally figured the man out.

A plate was set in front of Landon. Waterford piled food upon Landon's plate before he turned to his own. The waft of deliciously flavored meats and vegetables invaded Landon's thoughts, making his stomach rumble. He pressed a hand to his midriff. The elders served themselves one by one. Would they resume their inquisition or feast first?

In any other setting, as head PORF, Landon would be expected to initiate or decide what was to occur next. But he was quite comfortable waiting for the elders to act first. He basked in relief that, for now, he wasn't expected to be in charge. His decision to retain the rondure and hold the position of head PORF had opened his eyes to the distinctions between classes. Raised on the fringes of the upper class, he'd never pondered the archaic structure of society until he became head PORF. The Network was comprised of individuals from all classes. Still, over generations, the organization remained steadfast in its purpose to serve PORFs—nothing else mattered. They all shared the common goal and treated one another with the same respect. He glanced about the table. The council was a perfect example of how the Network functioned in harmony.

Two years of soul searching had left him exhausted but simultaneously excited for the future. His future father-in-law stared at him as if solving a puzzle of some sort. Landon had conducted himself to the best of his abilities during the adjustment period. Now, he would find out how others had viewed his progression.

Seated at the head of the table, Landon had a clear view of each member. He attempted to decipher which of the elders would act first. His posture remained defensive as he deflected the collective grim expressions sent his way. Waterford's attention was drawn to the massive pile of food on his plate. Oddly, he resisted consuming the delicious fare.

Mrs. Barnwell clasped her hands together in front of her and closed her eyes. The others followed suit, and he did too. But it was Mr. Cadby's voice that said, "Let's pray."

Landon peeked at the man who was to be his father-in-law. The same man who had tested Landon's patience, putting him through hours of discomfort as the mark of a PORF was placed upon him. Knowing Cadby's dislike of him, Landon was prepared to pay a king's ransom to gain the man's blessing. He never expected to want to win the man's respect, but now, Landon questioned whether he was even worthy of marrying one of the Network's most valued members.

"God, we thank ye for the blessed fare before us and pray for yer divine guidance in the matter before us today. Amen."

"Amen." Landon opened his eyes.

All the elders were poised to eat except for Cadby, who said, "What made ye decide to offer for me Bronwyn and not for a titled lady?"

Landon speared a slice of beef onto his fork and raised it to his mouth but then lowered it to his plate to answer. He had anticipated the question, but his pre-formulated answer didn't roll off his tongue as expected. Instead, he replied, "Bronwyn's beautiful features remain with me day and night. Her voice is..." Waterford's booted toe came into direct contact with his leg. He glared at the man, but seeing his friend's grin,

Landon realized waxing poetic phrases now would not gain him the council's blessings to marry Bronwyn. But his prepared speech would fail also. He'd have to employ his rusty barrister skills and form arguments as each question was posed, but with no prior cases to reference, he'd have to speak from the heart. "I wasn't raised to hold the title of earl, nor bear the honor of being the head PORF."

Cadby interrupted, "A titled lady could aid ye..."

Landon raised a hand to halt his future father-in-law. "If you will permit, I have a rather lengthy response." He glanced about the table. The elders nodded their consent to proceed, and Cadby stuffed his mouth full of food.

"The morn I asked Bronwyn for her hand in marriage, I had no clue she was a member of the Network. But I did know that she was an extraordinary woman. Intelligent and brave. As my secretary, she exhibited a quick mind and had provided me sound advice for years. She made me a better barrister." Landon clenched his stomach as it rumbled. The scent of the food tormented him, but winning the elders over was far more important. "Bronwyn does not back away from a challenge. When I told her she could not attend meetings with clients until her enunciation improved, she waltzed into my brother's office and demanded he assist her. She claimed since Christopher had hired her and told her she was capable of the position, it was his responsibility to train her. Bronwyn worked tirelessly to amend her accent."

"Aye, and we all suffered for it," Cadby muttered as

he chewed on a turkey leg. Even Mrs. Lennox nodded her head at Cadby's grumblings.

Ignoring the man's comment, Landon said, "I do not know of *any* unmarried, titled ladies who have the qualities I consider imperative for the Countess of Hadfield." Landon slid a glance to Waterford, who was grinning like a fool. "Bronwyn possesses the virtues I require. She is assertive, brave, compassionate, fair, gracious, and loyal. Should I go on?"

Before Landon could place the bite upon his fork in his mouth, Mrs. Barnwell said, "As a PORF, Bronwyn would lose the right to succeed Mr. Cadby on the council. Her brother Harold will assume the responsibility. We request Harold be trained in law so our members will continue to have access to the legal assistance that Bronwyn currently provides."

Cadby's features darkened. It was apparent he did not care for the change.

Landon replied, "I shall ensure Harold receives the best legal training and will confer with Bronwyn as to what her wishes and thoughts are with regard to the matter. What position does Harold currently hold?"

Every fork stilled. Were they shocked he'd discuss the matter with his wife or the fact he dared to pose a query of his own?

Waterford swallowed and whispered, "No questions."

Landon pushed his plate away from him. He wouldn't indulge until the proceedings were over. "Obviously, I'm here to address your concerns over my intention to marry Bronwyn." He shifted his gaze from one elder to the next as he spoke. "But unlike other potential suitors wishing to marry into the Network, I am a PORF. The head PORF. There hasn't been a PORF who has claimed possession of the rondure in generations. I've read journals from all three families, and I've yet to find guidance. But there is one fact that is blatantly clear, as the holder of the rondure, I am responsible for all PORFs *and* the Network." No one had moved during his entire monologue. He cringed at the thought behaving like a dictator, but PORFs and the Network needed to work together and cease to operate as two separate entities. "I apologize, Mrs. Barnwell, for interrupting the proceedings. I shall table my questions and concerns until after my return from Scotland."

Cadby's face turned bright red. Landon was about to stand and pound on the man's back when Waterford's hand fell upon his forearm and kept him in place.

"Scotland!" Cadby bellowed. "Coin or no coin, ye will have to prove to us tonight ye are worthy of wedding our Bronwyn."

Landon took a sip of his wine and faced Cadby's angry visage. "I'm willing to meet every one of your demands, answer any questions you may have, but no one will be leaving until I've received your blessing to wed Bronwyn."

The three ladies raised their goblets in the air, Landon followed suit, and then Waterford, Rutherford and Cadby did too.

Mrs. Barnwell toasted, "To new beginnings."

CHAPTER SIX

*T*he rhythm of the carriage horses' hooves hitting the cobbled road slowed, and Landon blinked away thoughts of a quick afternoon nap. He was accompanying Theo to Ms. Lennox's store for another fitting. Pregnancy had not slowed his cousin down in the slightest. The woman was always on the move and hard to corner, but he needed her assistance. Landon covered his umpteenth yawn. He was about to reach for the door latch when Theo cleared her throat. He paused and glanced at his cousin, who sat primly on the forward-facing seat with her hands firmly clasped in her lap.

Exhausted after no sleep for two consecutive nights, he leaned back. "What's the matter?"

Theo's emerald green eyes blazed with anger. "I don't understand why you insist on rushing off to Scotland. Archbroke obtained the special license you requested; why not have the ceremony here at week's end?"

"I simply changed my mind." He leaned forward to exit, but his cousin crossed her arms and glared at him. Obviously, Theo had more say on the issue and wasn't about to leave the carriage until she was satisfied.

"I don't believe you. You always have sound reasoning for every decision you make. Traveling to Scotland makes no sense."

Landon shrugged. "Hmm. And what would you say if I told you it was one of three concessions Bronwyn extracted before she agreed to marry me?"

Theo raised her hand and tapped a forefinger over her lips. "Clever. At least four days of travel time. An opportunity for the two of you to become reacquainted. And she's managed to avoid the prying eyes and gossip of the ton. An ingenious plan. Yes, as I said before, you've chosen wisely, cousin."

Theo's summation was enlightening. He hadn't taken time to analyze Bronwyn's demands; he'd simply been too busy ensuring he complied with them. Cadby was a keen negotiator, ensuring his daughter would be well cared for. Mrs. Barnwell had acted as a scribe, and he finally signed the marriage agreements as the first streaks of sunlight appeared.

Landon stared out the window at the modiste shop sign—the harped angel was cleverly interwoven into the design of a dress. Mrs. Lennox, mama to the proprietress, was extremely quiet during the negotiations, but when she did vocalize a demand on Bronwyn's behalf it was immediately noted without further discussion. While the council was supposed to be equally balanced among its members, Landon noted both Cadby's and Mrs. Lennox's wishes carried extra weight.

"How long does it typically take to assemble a trousseau?" Landon didn't want to incur Mrs. Lennox's wrath or spur the woman's ire by placing an undue burden on her daughter.

"I've not the slightest idea, but Emma is a miracle worker. Even with such short notice, I'm sure she has seen to it that Bronwyn will be well outfitted." Theo tugged on her gloves and adjusted her skirts.

Taking her cue, Landon opened the door and exited. He held out his hand to assist Theo, but despite her husband's concerns about a shift in the woman's center of gravity, his cousin's descent was as graceful as ever.

Before Theo reached the front door, Landon reached out and tapped her on the shoulder. He needed her help on a matter. There was little time left before he and Bronwyn set off for Scotland, and he hadn't met all of the council's demands. While it was unlike him to waffle, he also didn't make important decisions on a whim. Landon sighed and asked, "What would be an appropriate wedding gift for Bronwyn?"

Theo twisted at the waist. "Aside from the preliminary reports I've managed to obtain, all of which were extremely complimentary, I've no knowledge of your bride." She searched his features and said, "Not to worry. Fortunately, we are visiting Emma. She's reported to be Bronwyn's dearest friend. I shall make inquires, and

Morris will see to it that a gift is packed along with your belongings."

At his nod, she turned back and entered the quaint establishment. The bell over the door rang, announcing their arrival. Landon tucked his hands behind his back and shifted to the nearest corner. The shop was surprisingly spacious and appeared to provide multiple services in addition to dressmaking. Bolts of material he would have expected to find at the linen-drapers were stacked about the room. Ribbon and lace one would generally find in a haberdashery peeked out of one of the drawers built into a large table in the center of the room. How clever of Ms. Lennox to combine and offer all the related services.

A honey-blonde woman similar in age to Bronwyn appeared.

Theo stepped up onto the platform. "I'm not sure how you are going to hide the bump." His cousin ran a hand over her rounded belly. "Can you fathom, no one has even made mention of my fuller figure."

The woman snorted. "Lady Theo, I can assure ye, that's not me doin'."

Landon chuckled. Not a single member of the ton or the Network was willing to incur Archbroke's wrath by upsetting Theo. The man was renowned for inflicting the most heinous punishments if disobeyed.

Theo's suspicious glare landed upon him. Landon stood up straight and shook his head. "Don't look at me. I'm not involved."

"Humph." Theo ran her hand over her slightly

rounded hips. "If it wasn't you, then the fault lies with my beloved husband. Oh, how rude of me." Theo hopped down from the platform, rushed over, and extracted him from the corner. "Landon, this is Emma, Ms. Lennox. Emma, this is my cousin, Landon Neale, Lord Hadfield, and soon to be your best friend's husband."

Emma curtsied. "It's an honor to meet ye, Lord Hadfield, and please call me Emma."

"Then you must address me as Landon. I'm pleased to meet a close friend of Bronwyn's."

The modiste ushered Theo back up onto the platform. "I heard ye met me mum last night. Me sisters said she didn't come home until the wee hours of the morn. Must have been some meetin'." Like Bronwyn, Emma was direct.

"It was quite the experience," Landon admitted.

"Well, the lads are loadin' up the coach." Emma waved her hands as she talked. "Ye didn't give me much time, but Bronwyn will be ready for any event."

Despite Emma's lively tone, there was an undercurrent of displeasure. Revealing his dimple, Landon said. "I apologize, Emma, for such short notice. Please allow me to compensate you for the inconvenience."

"Oh, me price ain't coin. Oh no, that would be too easy for ye."

Landon ignored Theo's giggle in the background.

Damn. He wasn't going to be able to charm his way out of this. "Name your price." It was like he was negotiating all over again for Bronwyn's hand.

"Hmmm...let me fink." Emma placed her hands on

her hips and turned to Theo and then back to him. "All right, I reckon ye'd agree to pay me anythin' I ask for. But I love me Bronwyn more than anythin' I need. All I ask of ye is to be patient with her. She might be smart and knows her p's and q's, but she's blind and can't see herself."

Landon blinked. "Beg pardon? Blind?"

"Ye, know...she..." Emma swiveled to and looked to Theo for help.

Theo explained, "Cousin, Emma wants you to help Bronwyn discover her own self-worth."

Hip cocked to one side, Emma waited for his answer.

Landon nodded. "I shall try my best to honor your request."

Apparently satisfied by his response, Emma led Theo through a doorway and disappeared.

What had he done? How was he to aid Bronwyn in her discovery of self-worth when he hadn't managed to find his own? Two years of turmoil had him questioning his capabilities and, at times, wishing he'd never inherited the damn earldom and the PORF family legacy.

Brow furrowed, he went to the store window and watched as footmen loaded one trunk after another onto the carriage. Not once since receiving the mark had he needed to see to the finer points of his travel plans. The Network worked like a well-oiled machine; everyone worked in unison for one purpose, ensuring the PORFs had every necessary resource to do their duties. He reached into his pocket, and his fingers grazed the edge of the rondure that symbolized his responsibility to the other PORFs and the entire Network. Every day he questioned whether or not he was worthy of holding such a position. Perhaps he and Bronwyn had more in common than he initially surmised. A warmth spread through his chest—yes, he had chosen wisely. All he had to do was convince his bride to be.

CHAPTER SEVEN

*L*ying on her side, snuggled under her covers precariously close to the edge of the bed, Bronwyn waited for the sound of her mum padding down the hall to start the day. Her mum was always the first to wake and the last to bed. Most of the night, Bronwyn's mind was awhirl and sleep eluded her. Never having had a reason to become acquainted with any ladies of the ton, her knowledge of their customs was purely second hand and restricted to those within the Network who served in PORF households. The fashionable ladies would never deem her suitable to attend their afternoon teas.

Irritated with her train of thought, Bronwyn shifted. Her sister's knobby knee poked her in the middle of her back. What would it be like to sleep without three other warm bodies in the bed? She'd shared a bed with her sisters all her life. The thought of sleeping as titled ladies were reported to do, alone and vulnerable, sent shivers down Bronwyn's spine. Her husband would sleep behind a closed connecting door instead of next to her. How very remote. Her parents never slept apart even when her mum was irate at her dad. In less than a week, Lord Hadfield would be her husband. Not Landon Neale, the dashing barrister she once worked alongside, who caused her pulse to race as he rattled off case law, but an earl who secretly served the Crown. Bronwyn tugged the sheets up to her chin. Her mind continued to spin. Of all the women in London, why had Landon chosen her?

The chamber door softly creaked open. Barely opening her eyes, Bronwyn feigned sleep. Her mum snuck into the room with the most stunning traveling gown she had ever seen. Emma was indeed the most talented seamstress in town. Having never worn such elegant attire, Bronwyn clutched at the sheets. She wasn't ready. This wasn't the future she had envisioned.

Her mum leaned down and brushed back the hair from her face. "Love. It's time."

"I don't want to go. He's made a mistake in asking me."

"Hush. Lord Hadfield knows what he's about." Her mum placed a kiss upon her temple. "Your dad and I are very proud of ye."

She wasn't a youngling. She was five and twenty—plenty old enough not to need her ma's coddling. Bronwyn slipped her feet out of the covers onto the cold wood floor, padded over to the corner, and leaned over the washbasin. The cold water upon her face fortified her spirits. She had never failed to be a fully contributing member of her family or the Network, and she wasn't about to start.

Sally, her youngest sibling, scrambled from the bed. "Mum, can I go with Bronwyn and be her lady's maid?"

"Git back into bed. It's way too early for ye to be up. There are three qualified maids awaiting Bronwyn downstairs."

Bronwyn wiped her face with a clean linen. "Who's down below?"

"Little Tilman, young Carrington, and Willa Peyton. You must select one of them to accompany ye. They will travel along with Lord Hadfield's valet."

All of the girls her mum mentioned were close to Bronwyn in age. The glaring reality of the situation had her mind reeling. She could have been selected to apply for the position of lady's maid and bodyguard to Landon's wife. Instead, she was to be his wife. She wasn't any better than the three girls below. Was it pure happenstance?

Bronwyn considered her options. Tilman and Carrington's older sisters served Lady Grace and Lady Lucy. Both would have excellent insight into being a lady's maid. They would also easily identify Bronwyn's shortcomings and missteps. She didn't want her non-ladylike behavior shared with other households, plus Bronwyn considered Willa a friend. Willa was mature, trustworthy, and had a solid head upon her shoulders. It would also elevate Willa's family within the Network if she served the head PORF's wife.

With a decisive nod, Bronwyn said, "Willa is my

choice."

Her mum's smile was that of pure pride. "I shall go fetch her now." Embracing Bronwyn in a quick hug, her mum added, "A fine decision, and the first of many to come."

An hour later, Bronwyn stepped out her front door to face her fiancé. Landon straightened away from the large, crested traveling coach but remained loose-limbed as he revealed bright white teeth and his irresistible dimple. The vehicle was impressive but not in comparison to the man standing next to it. Dressed in a dark blue waistcoat, pristine white lawn shirt, tan breeches, and a conservatively tied cravat, Landon was dashing, to say the least. The man was totally at ease and eager to begin their journey—the stark opposite of Bronwyn, who was a bundle of nerves and reservations.

Bronwyn curtsied. "I apologize for the delay, my lord."

"No need to apologize. Theo and my mama have me well trained in the art of waiting on a lady." The corner of his lips shifted, highlighting his roguish dimple. Sweeping a hand in the direction of the coach, he said, "I think it best if you call me Landon, don't you?"

Bronwyn stared at the charming, relaxed man before her. Who was he? She was accustomed to the no-nonsense, matter-of-fact Landon. Bronwyn inhaled sharply as the realization that her request to travel to

Scotland, born from her desire to become better acquainted with her betrothed, placed her in extremely close quarters with the man whose smile turned her knees weak and elevated her body temperature to uncomfortable levels.

Landon entered the coach close behind her. It was physically impossible to feel the heat of him through the many layers of clothing she had donned this morn, but her cheeks were flushed, and her entire body was over-heated. Bronwyn adjusted her skirts as she sat upon the plush, forward-facing seat. She inhaled sharply as she took in the well-padded bench across from her, the interior lights, and the fine material covering the windows. This was no hackney.

Landon searched her features as he settled onto the rear-facing seat. "Is anything the matter?"

"No. It's just Emma fashioned the traveling gown out of heavy velvet. I'm unaccustomed to such warmth."

"I can wait if you care to change. We have a long day of travel ahead of us. It's best you are comfortable."

"Oh, no. I promise I won't be bothersome."

Landon's brows snapped into a frown. "When I alter my decisions, do you find me *bothersome*?"

Without thinking, she replied, "Well, yes." She bent her head and shook it. "What I mean is..."

Affronted but curious, Landon said, "Yes?"

"It's our duty to serve you to the best of our capabilities, and when you change directions, it sometimes means people have wasted time and effort. We hate to disappoint you, or any of the other PORFs, for that matter."

"Do you fear you will disappoint me as a wife?"

Bronwyn twisted her hands, bunching her skirts in her lap. "Yes."

"Let me ask you this before I give the order to leave. Do you wish to marry me, or have you agreed out of duty?"

How was she to answer? She wasn't in love with him, nor did she expect him to be in love with her. While she had a strong physical attraction to the man, it hadn't been the reason she agreed to wed him.

Landon sighed. "That was unfair of me to ask." He drummed his fingers upon his knee. That habit indicated he was considering changing his mind.

A rush of anxiety rolled through her. "It is my wish."

"Why?"

"Beg pardon?"

Landon arched one eyebrow. "Why do you wish to marry me?"

Blast. He had caught her unprepared. She'd have to list the traits she was aware he possessed and hope it would be sufficient to appease his curiosity.

"You are intelligent, honorable, and steadfast." She clasped her hands in her lap and smiled up at him. "You take your responsibilities seriously and rule with fairness." It wasn't so hard to explain her admiration for him after all. "You care and protect your family with a fierceness that I find endearing."

A blush rose in his cheeks as she continued to rattle off compliments.

"I suppose marriages have been founded on less." He

lifted his heel and stamped three times. The carriage rocked forward as the horses were set into motion.

Did she dare ask the same question of him? She wasn't certain she wanted to know the answer, so she'd wait for another opportunity to ask.

Landon turned to look out the carriage window, and she did likewise. Streaks of sunlight glinted off shop windows as they rolled onto the main thoroughfare.

"Do you not fear I will be an embarrassment to you amongst the ton?"

"Pfft. I care nothing for the opinion of the ton." He continued to stare out the window. "Mama, Theo, and Christopher all agree—I've made a sage decision."

"I've not met either your mama or Lady Theo."

"Apparently, my brother has supplied my mama with enough details that she believes in her heart that you are perfect for me. Theo has her own sources and is extremely excited for our return and to make your acquaintance." Landon chuckled and then turned to face her. "Some might say she ordered me to present you to her posthaste. Which I'll happily do as soon as we are in accord."

"Are we in disaccord, my lord?"

"Aye, as you aren't comfortable yet calling me by my Christian name. But I hope to rectify the situation by the time we arrive in Gretna Green."

Oh, how she wished she'd managed to sleep the night prior. Landon had a sharp mind and was a master at disarming his witnesses. She'd need to keep her guard up and wits about her at all times.

CHAPTER EIGHT

our years studying law at university and six
years of cross-examinations in court had not
provided Landon with the skills necessary to break down
Bronwyn's defenses. Emma was wise to ask him to be
patient. For two days, Bronwyn steadfastly refused to
give him any glimpse into the passionate woman he
suspected lay beneath the remote exterior. They traveled
in easy companionship, but as soon as a topic that
bordered on a personal nature arose, Bronwyn would
tactfully redirect their conversation.

His fiancée blinked as she rose from a nap. She'd
been fitful in her sleep, and Landon had carefully repositioned her in order for her to rest her head comfortably
upon his shoulder.

"Landon?"

"Yes, my dear." He fantasized about kissing her again,
but she hadn't shown any interest in repeating the act
that kept him semi aroused.

She sat up abruptly. "I'm so sorry."

"Why are you apologizing?" He caressed her cheek, where the seam of his coat had left an indentation. "As your fiancé, it is my duty to see to your comfort and needs."

The flare of interest he'd been hoping for blazed in her blue eyes. Landon trailed a finger down her neck and along her collar bone. Her breath hitched.

Bronwyn's gaze fixed on his mouth. Was she waiting for him to kiss her?

He leaned in and gently pressed his lips to hers. She released a moan that prompted him to trail his tongue along the seam of her lips. She parted her lips, and the desire to devour her was overwhelming. From years of working alongside her, Landon had learned Bronwyn was a quick study, but the enchanting shift of her lips against his had him eager to explore and discover which of his caresses would send her over the edge. Would she entrust him with her body? There was but one way to find out.

He pulled back slightly. Bronwyn was not ready to end the kiss. She pressed closer, extracting a deep growl from him as she reclaimed his mouth. He eased his tongue back into her mouth to explore and then began to withdraw. She surprised him as she captured his tongue between her lips. Oh. How he wanted her lips to circle other parts of his anatomy.

Nibbling on her neck, Landon mumbled, "If you continue to kiss me that way, we'll have to cut our journey short and wed by special license."

Bronwyn hooked her arms around his neck and guided his head back to her. Rather than reclaiming her rosy lips, he dipped his head lower and licked the valley between her breasts. Bronwyn's sharp gasp was followed by a sweet purr. She edged forward, rocking her hips closer to him. As if connected, his body mimicked her movements. Ignoring the raging need to explore further, Landon grunted as he loosened his hold. He wasn't about to take Bronwyn for the first time in a bloody coach. His body rebelled at his morality.

Short of breath, she asked, "How much longer until we reach Scotland?"

"We've merely begun our journey. At least another three or four days."

Bronwyn straightened and sat, staring wide-eyed at him. "Three days?"

"At least."

Bronwyn's brow creased into a frown, but her eyes were bright, still lit with desire.

"I promise I'll do whatever necessary to see to your comfort."

Her lips twisted into a smirk. "You promise?"

Her cheeks were flushed, and her lips beckoned for kisses. He'd agree to anything at that moment. Landon swallowed hard and nodded. "On one condition...you have to tell me specifically what causes you discomfort."

It was Bronwyn's turn to swallow hard.

She slid her hand over his shoulder and began kneading the back of his neck. Her touch melted some of his anxiety over her answer. Leaning forward, she flicked his earlobe once before capturing it between her lips. Damn, the woman had learned his preferences fast. With a groan, he pushed her back, placing another inch of distance between them.

He needed her agreement first. He wanted all of her —both heart and body.

Firm but gentle, he said, "I need you to tell me, not show me."

"But...but I'm not sure what...how to describe my discomfort." Her eyes fluttered closed.

He couldn't give in. "Please. Try."

His heart sank as Bronwyn sat back and busied herself, adjusting her skirts from side to side. He had ruined the moment. But there was too much at stake. If he was to fulfill his promise to Bronwyn's best friend Emma, he needed to discover Bronwyn's thoughts. The best way to achieve that was to gain her trust and have her share with him her feelings and opinions ranging from the trivial to intimate details like he had just requested.

Back stiff, she leaned back against the cushioned coach bench. "I want to tell you...but I've not the words." She wiggled her hips. With a side glance, she lowered her gaze to his breeches that were tented.

Perhaps he was asking too much of an innocent. "Would you like me to assist with suggestions?"

"Please." Her eager tone was encouraging. He might be able to salvage this leg of the trip after all. He twisted and scooted back into the corner.

He wrapped his arm around her back and tugged her

to his side. "Relax." Without hesitation, she did as he asked. His heart fluttered at the small indication of pure trust.

He wasn't certain how to begin. Balancing his two objectives would be difficult. "Shall I share with you my discomfort?"

Damnation. What had he been thinking of positioning them where he could not read her features?

"Your discomfort was obvious, my lord, but you cannot observe mine." Bronwyn's teasing set the tone of his reply.

"Ah, but you are wrong, my dear." He raised his hand to cup her breast. "I saw your taut nipples." He ran his thumb over the pebbled bump in the material, and the gentle push against his hand was all the encouragement he needed to continue his exploration. "They've ached for attention from the moment I tasted you." He slid a finger between the valley of her breasts. The back of his hand brushed against the soft velvet material of her gown.

Bronwyn's hand covered his, their fingers interlaced. She said, "Your caresses cause sensations that are befuddling. I simultaneously want..."

Landon squeezed her nipple between one of his and her fingers. His actions elicited a moan of pure pleasure that, in turn, sent a surge of desire straight to his loins. To ease the ache, he shifted to settle Bronwyn comfortably against his chest. With his left hand, he gathered up handfuls of material until he had hiked up her skirt high enough to slip his hand over her thigh. He pushed her garter and silk stocking down until his palm rested against her warm skin.

Tracing the curve of her ear with his tongue, Landon inched his fingers closer to her slit. He said, "I must confess most of my uneasiness centers between my legs, but my heart beats erratically, and my thoughts are scattered. I can't decide where I want to touch you the most."

Bronwyn's head rolled to the side, allowing full access to her beautiful neck.

On a half sigh, half moan Bronwyn replied, "My skin is hot. I'm damp between my legs, and my breasts feel heavy."

His lips curved into a smile as he settled them upon her neck. Torn between settling for her description of her physical discomfort and the need to extract more from her, he gave her a gentle bite. "Is that all?"

She wiggled her hips. Landon's finger dipped lower and was coated in warm, delicious wetness. He wanted to withdraw his hand and put his finger in his mouth, eager to find out what she would taste like.

"No, my lord, that is not all." Bronwyn's breathy response halted his hand's retreat. "I've secretly imagined you stealing a kiss or two over the years, which caused a fluttering in my heart. But your kisses...they do much more than create a flutter. They generate a much deeper ache."

Oh, how he desperately wanted to ease her ache and make love to her. But for now, he would reward her bravery and honesty. He slid his finger along the wet slit between her thighs.

He whispered, "Open for me, love."

Again, without hesitation, Bronwyn obeyed and spread her legs.

"Wider." Eyes closed, he mentally visualized himself kneeling between her thighs at the ready to taste her. He moved his fingers, mimicking the motions his tongue would perform one day soon.

Arching her back, Bronwyn clenched her hand that remained atop his, over her breast. Even as a child, he was a skilled multitasker, able to rub his tummy and pat his head at the same time. In adulthood, that talent had translated into the ability to finger a woman while he simultaneously fondled, pinched, and teased her breast until she reached her peak. Circling the tender nub at her center with his left hand, he moved his right to Bronwyn's neglected breast. Landon flicked the nipple to attention, and Bronwyn writhed against him. The curve of her bottom brushed against his hard member. He eased a finger into her channel and used his thumb to press and circle the sensitive skin above her entrance.

Rotating her hips, Bronwyn released moan after moan.

He withdrew his finger and tapped the swollen nub at her core. "Do you like that?"

"Aaa...aha..."

She jutted her hips as his fingers slapped against her. The thrill of learning Bronwyn's preferences spurred him to continue. He alternated between sliding a finger into her and light taps.

"Hmm..."

Her purrs of pleasure continued. Bronwyn's inner muscles clamped tighter as he slid a second finger into her already stretched and ready channel. Sensing she was close to reaching her peak, Landon pumped his fingers, inching deeper until his palm laid flat against her. Seconds later, her back arched and she stiffened. He twisted to cover her mouth with his as she cried out in pleasure. Reluctantly he released her sweet lips, but he continued stroke his wife-to-be until her pulsating muscles relaxed and her body collapsed against his.

His own breathing was ragged and labored. Landon withdrew his hand and licked his fingers. "Hmm..."

Wide-eyed, Bronwyn asked, "You enjoy the taste of me?"

"Aye, and I can't wait to taste you properly." The woman was a blend of sweet and salty and he was eager to experience the flavor fully.

She swiveled and leaned back against his chest. With a curt nod she said, "I too am looking forward to it."

Landon chuckled. *Aye.* The devilishly smart minx was a fast study.

Removing his hand from her chest, he adjusted himself without success. He'd have to refrain from touching Bronwyn and hope his body would relax. His fiancée had other ideas. She pressed closer and snuggled against his side. He rested the back of his head against the coach wall and recited the alphabet in French, German and Latin.

LANDON BLINKED HIS EYES OPEN. He must have dozed off.

Bronwyn had her arms wound tightly about his waist. Now that she had trusted him with her body, would she trust him with her emotions?

As the day came to an end, he gently shook Bronwyn awake. "We shall be arriving at the coaching inn soon."

With a broad smile, she peered up at him. "Do you think this one might have a hip bath available?"

The day before, they had arrived late at the Network inn, and Bronwyn hadn't wanted to add to the staff's duties. Neither Peyton nor she were accustomed to traveling and had fallen fast asleep in one of the two rooms Landon had reserved for their stay.

"I shall see to it that one is brought up for you."

"Will you always be accommodating, or once we are married, will the staid, proper Landon return?"

Staid and proper. Ha. If she were a mind reader, she'd have known years ago his thoughts were anything but gentlemanly. He asked, "Which version do you prefer?"

"I'll admit at first I was caught off guard, finding myself betrothed to a rogue..."

"A rogue? I don't believe I've ever..."

Bronwyn shifted, and her hand came to rest on his thigh, halting his speech.

"Not literally. I'd never believe you to be dishonest or a scoundrel, but in the vein that you were behaving most unpredictably."

"Unpredictable?"

Her cheek brushed against his chest as she nodded. "Yes. Or perhaps a better descriptor would be impulsive."

"My dear, apparently, my mind remains foggy from your kisses. I'm not following." He wasn't exaggerating. Her innocent movements were playing havoc with his body and mind.

"Your actions have been contrary to what I'd come to expect from you. The man I spent the better part of every day with, assisting in preparing court arguments and dissertations, would never act rashly."

Had his behavior altered that noticeably over the past two years? He waited, and when she finally peered up at him, Landon said, "Please outline for me what behaviors I exhibited that were out of character."

"With pleasure. First, you proposed to *me*, of all people. Second, you acquiesced to my demands without any real attempt to negotiate. Third, your kisses make my toes curl in my shoes."

A chuckle bubbled up from his chest. "Let me reiterate once again my reasoning for proposing to you, Bronwyn Cadby. Apparently, I've made a hash of my prior two attempts." He didn't take his eyes off her. "For the past two years, since I inherited the Hadfield title, there has only been one woman who entered my thoughts daily, and that is you." He gave her a quick kiss to punctuate his statement. "There is no other who knows me as well as you do, nor one as brave as you to marry a PORF." He grabbed her hand and brought it up to his chest. "You have stated that I'm oblivious as to who you really are, yet you have rebuffed my every effort these past days to become better acquainted with you."

She curled her fingers into his. "I shall promise to be forthright with you if you promise to remain the rogue who kisses me unexpectedly."

He tugged her closer. "You have my word."

The coach door handle rattled.

Bronwyn pulled away and ran a hand over her mussed coiffure. "How do I look?"

"Perfect."

"You are a terrible liar. Your dimple gives you away every time." Bronwyn lifted her skirts as the coach door opened—a footman stood ready to assist her.

The woman did know him well. He needed to convince his fiancée that he knew her just as well. He could recall every minute detail of her features and mannerisms. But if questioned about her likes and dislikes, he might need to make further inquiries. He did know, with absolute certainty, she enjoyed his kisses and caresses.

CHAPTER NINE

*P*erched precariously on the coach bench, Bronwyn wrapped her arms about her midsection and gasped for air between bursts of laughter.

Landon's forehead was scrunched and his lips drawn into a tight line, his attempt at imitating Mr. Rutherford.

Gasping for air, Bronwyn pleaded, "Stop. You must stop; my stomach aches."

She rolled back, and Landon caught the back of her head before it hit the wall of the coach. His impressions of various members of the Network were on point.

Her fiancé had kept the mood light the entire day as if Landon had sensed her growing apprehension toward arriving in Scotland. For the past three days they shared both serious and humorous stories of their upbringing. Landon, in turn, had kept his promise and provided her with kisses at the most unexpected moments.

As they neared their destination, her fear of failing him grew. He was a remarkable man who needed an extraordinary woman for a wife. Not a shopkeeper's daughter who happened to be born with a mind for debate and a tongue that longed for the taste of him. Despite his reassurances that she was the wife he wanted, the persistent suspicion that she wasn't good enough for him waged a war upon her confidence.

Landon gripped her hand. "Are you nervous?"

"Aren't you?"

He shook his head. "I've no concerns about marrying you."

Landon reached into his coat pocket and pulled out the rondure and a shiny ring with a unique stone in the center. Landon slipped the coin back into his pocket. The freedom to be herself over the past few days had lulled her into believing he was simply a man ready to wed. But in truth, Landon was an extremely wealthy and powerful man in need of a wife. How could he have no misgivings about marrying her?

She didn't believe love was required to make a marriage successful, but as the days had passed, she had begun to wish for him to utter the foolish words. He desired her, as she lusted for him. Was it enough?

Landon reached for her hand. "This ring is for you, a symbol of my true intentions. But before I give it to you, I want you to know that while it is my wish to marry you, I will not force you or order you to marry me." He placed the ring in the center of her palm and closed her fingers over it. "If you decide to wear it, I'll know you believe me when I say there is no other woman for me." He placed a chaste kiss upon her hand

and exited the travel coach, leaving the door open behind him.

Landon was no liar; if she decided to change her decision, he'd most likely ensure the blame fell upon him. She opened her hand and peered at the ring. Exquisite pink gems surrounded her birthstone.

Willa peeked her head in. "Is something the matter?"

She needed a moment to think—alone. Clutching the ring tight in her hand, she shifted her skirts about. "I can't come out, there's a tear in the side of my gown." The lie rolled off her tongue, and she immediately regretted it.

"Not to worry. I'll fetch you a coat." Willa disappeared.

For the first time since Landon's initial proposal, Bronwyn believed that the decision to marry was solely hers. Previously she had amassed arguments for and against marrying a titled gentleman who happened to also be a PORF. This time, she swiftly ran through the advantages and disadvantages of marrying Landon, the version of the man she'd come to know during their journey.

A great coat appeared in the doorway. Bronwyn's hand trembled as she slipped the ring onto her finger—a perfect fit. With a burst of warmth in her heart, Bronwyn rose and exited the coach. Feet on the ground, and the coat was wrapped about her shoulders. Landon's scent tickled her nose.

In a teasing tone, her betrothed said, "Last chance to change your mind."

She linked her arm through his and rested her hand

upon his forearm. Bronwyn tapped her finger and was pleased to see Landon's dimple appear as he caught sight of the ring. She grinned and said, "You shall be stuck with me for life."

"Wonderful." He leaned down and gave her a quick kiss before all and sundry. "The innkeeper is ready whenever you are."

Willa nervously stood in front of them, blocking their way. "My lord. Bronwyn—" Willa shook her head at her mistake and then continued, "I mean *my mistress* is not yet ready. Emma will kill me if Bronwyn doesn't wear the bridal gown that she labored on all night."

It was going to take some time for Willa, like herself, to adjust to their new positions, but together they would muddle through.

Landon smiled, but his devilish dimple failed to appear. "We wouldn't want to cause Emma upset now, would we? I shall wait."

Hauled into the cozy inn, which appeared to be connected to a blacksmith shop, Bronwyn gave into Willa's every demand. Her friend, now maid, tugged, pulled and pushed every strand upon her head until her scalp ached.

Bronwyn exhaled the last particle of air that remained in her lungs as Willa tied her stays strings tight. "I suppose I'll have to address you as Peyton after I'm married."

"And I shall refer to you as my lady."

Bronwyn raised her hand and stuck out her little finger in the air. "Only in the company of others?"

Willa shook her head. "We've been friends ever since we were children, and we shall always remain friends. I'm honored you chose me, but if I'm to succeed, I need you to become the lady I know you are."

Blast! Why did Willa have to always speak the truth? Bronwyn should have known there would be drawbacks to having a trusted friend as a maid. Willa was right. By day's end, she would become Countess Hadfield, and she had best learn to behave like a lady and quickly. First, she'd start by thinking and referring to her friend as Peyton.

Peyton bent down and removed a simple white gown with an intricate white lace overlay from one of her traveling trunks.

Bronwyn gaped at the dress. Emma's creation was splendid.

Peyton held up the dress to her body and spun. "It's the adult version of the white shift we used to wear when play-acting as children."

"Aye, except it was Emma who always wore the dress, and I wore breeches."

They both giggled as Peyton assisted Bronwyn into the dress.

As each button slipped into place, Bronwyn's anxiety increased. What if she made a hash of their wedding night?

"Peyton."

"Yes, my lady."

"Do *you* know how consummation occurs?"

Her friend blushed bright red. "Ah. Didn't your mum explain?"

"We didn't have time to discuss much of anything before I left. And you know how tough it is to obtain privacy in my house."

Peyton's brow creased. "Remember the time we saw the horses playing in the meadow?"

"Aye. But that's not what I'm inquiring about. I understand what must go where and such. What I want to know is how am I to please him. He needs me to produce an heir." Bronwyn began to pace as she continued with her concerns. "I'm well aware that it might require the act to be repeated. How do I ensure he'll want to...well, you know."

Hands-on her hips, Peyton asked, "Why do you believe I'd know the answer?"

"You have five older brothers. Both you and Emma have had a series of beaus while I've had none. Plus, you're my maid, and so you are supposed to have all the answers."

A burst of laughter escaped Peyton, and she bent at the waist. "I've been your maid for less than a week. My brothers are useless sources of information. Besides a few stolen kisses, I've not a clue as to what occurs between husband and wife. However, I am determined to be an excellent maid. While you get hitched, I'll make inquires and report back when you return."

"I knew I could count on you. I'd never have been able to ask anyone else about such matters."

Peyton gave her a hug. "I'll always be here for you."

"And I for you." Bronwyn pulled back to ask, "Now that you are part of the Hadfield staff, do you think your brothers will be less likely to scare off possible suitors?"

"Not likely. Regardless of our new positions, or the new world we will be thrust in, the Network will always protect and shelter us." Peyton turned her about to face the door. "If I were to find someone mad enough to marry me willingly, the poor sod would still have to seek out my dad and brothers' approvals, and if he wasn't already a member of the Network, he'd have to seek out permission from the elders."

Midstride, Bronwyn swiveled to face Peyton. The elders were a protective bunch. Had Landon sought out permission from the elders? He needn't have. Peyton's chuckles broke her train of thought.

With a knowing smile, Peyton said, "Lord Hadfield didn't have to seek anyone's approval. As head of the PORFs, the man can do as he pleases. But I heard he did meet with your dad and the Network elders and was given a good roasting. Only after a long night of negotiations did they give him their approval to marry you."

"He did that all for me?"

"My lady, I believe Lord Hadfield is smitten with you. He gave into nearly every demand the elders made in order to have you as his wife."

Bronwyn shook her head. Why would Landon do such a thing?

Her maid brushed the back of her finger over the top of her cheekbone. "You are worthy of his love."

Was she?

CHAPTER TEN

*T*ired of pacing in his room, Landon ventured downstairs.

Addair approached, eyeing Landon's traveling desk. "Lord Hadfield, allow me to escort you to the private parlor."

"My thanks, Mr. Addair, but I'd prefer to be seated where I may promptly greet my bride as soon as she descends."

The innkeeper shooed patrons from a trestle table that would afford Landon a clear view of the stairs. "Here ye go, Lord Hadfield."

Landon slid onto the bench, flipping his tailcoat out. With practiced movements, he arranged his writing equipment and sheets of parchment. During the last two years, Landon had spent more time traveling by coach than he ever had in his life. Traveling between London, the two crumbling country estates he'd inherited, and the Continent to locate the rondure, Landon had seen more of the world than he ever expected to. He'd been pleased with his lot in life before inheriting the Hadfield title from Theo's papa. However, the idea of scurrying between his office and court no longer held the appeal it once did. His uncle had left the Hadfield estate in near ruin, but the challenge of refilling the family coffers and learning the generations-old duty as a PORF opened Landon's eyes to a life he'd not known—one he now relished.

"If there's nothin' else ye need, my lord, I'm off to check to make sure everything is readied." Bronwyn had requested Addair, a longtime member of the Network, conduct the ceremony rather than the local blacksmith.

Landon absent-mindedly nodded as he began to draft a reply to Archbroke. Having recently attended a series of weddings, Landon was unperturbed by what was to occur next. Granted, none of them were a handfasting or conducted over an anvil, but how different could it really be?

Letter in hand, he looked up when a shadow fell over the table.

Bronwyn. Dressed in a stunning white gown that was obviously designed for her and only her. It fitted snugly across the chest with an intricate lace overlay. Squinting, he made out little harped angels woven into the material —the symbol used by the Network. She smiled down at him.

She boldly approached with her hands clasped behind her back. Mere inches away, she said, "I see you're busy. Should I return to my room and wait?"

Landon quickly stood up. His head swam. "No. No. I wasn't sure how long you would be. Nerves were getting the better of me, so I decided to take care of a few matters while I waited."

He scanned the room, which was completely empty. Jacobs was to alert him when Bronwyn had left her room. Where was his valet?

Landon's fear she would change her mind at the last minute faded as Bronwyn's lips curved into a smile. He fumbled the first button of his coat as his wife-to-be ran her top teeth over her bottom lip. Lips that would be forever his after this day. As each button slipped into place, Landon's apprehension of departing this world early eased. In marrying Bronwyn, he would secure the future of the PORFs and establish a critical link to the Network.

He stepped out over the bench to stand beside Bronwyn. "Shall we find Jacobs and Peyton?"

"They are already waiting for us, along with Mr. Addair."

"Where?"

"I believe we are to meet Mr. Addair at the smithy."

Damnation. He should have requested more specifics from Addair. Holding in a deep sigh, he winged his arm for his fiancée. Bronwyn placed her hand on his arm, and together they walked out of the inn and into a surprisingly fine sunny day.

His heart skipped a beat at Bronwyn's relaxed and poised features. He'd imagined her while he was busy adjusting to his new responsibilities, but fantasies failed to measure up to the woman standing beside him. Bronwyn peered up through her eyelashes, catching him gawking at her décolleté. Her cheeks flushed pink, but she flashed a lopsided smirk before she bowed her head.

As he placed his hand over Bronwyn's upon his arm, warmth seeped through his veins. Worries about her willingness to marry drifted away on the soft breeze that tickled the back of his neck. He'd been so busy admiring Bronwyn they were already midway across the open thoroughfare before his footsteps faltered. He had failed to mention how lovely she was or share how lucky he deemed himself to have her as wife.

Bronwyn's head swiveled to take in their surroundings. There was an undercurrent of energy. Landon tensed. Past the stables and the coaching house, a large crowd had gathered around the anvil.

Instead of complimenting Bronwyn, Landon's thoughts tumbled out in a grumble. "We only need two witnesses, not the entire town."

"I'd wager most are not locals. Some may have traveled a fair distance, at their own expense mind you, to witness our wedding. It's a rare opportunity for the likes of them to attend an auspicious event such as this."

Had this been part of Bronwyn's plan to allow members of the Network an opportunity to partake in the celebrations? When he assumed the role of head PORF, Landon had set out to find a way to bridge the gap between PORFs and those who served them. Initially, he'd believed it a stroke of good luck that he'd proposed to a valued member of the Network, but in hindsight, it wasn't luck. It was fate.

The crowd parted to make way for them to pass. A murmur of oohs and ahhs rose in a gentle wave as Bronwyn walked past. His chest puffed out with pride. He was a fortunate man, indeed.

Mr. Addair spotted them approaching and rushed up. "My lord, please follow me."

Dutifully following the innkeeper, he and Bronwyn smiled at the onlookers.

They stopped in front of an anvil housed at the back of the smithy, under a partial roof, and next to a hot stove.

Mr. Addair waved Peyton and Jacobs closer. Once they stood next to Bronwyn, Mr. Addair grabbed a long walking stick and dragged it to etch a circle in the ground with Bronwyn and Landon in the center. Once the two ends met, he outlined a winding pattern of laurel leaves. Handing the stick off to a bystander, Mr. Addair asked, "Are you ready to begin?"

Bronwyn nodded, and Landon replied, "Aye."

Peyton handed the innkeeper a strip of white silk that matched Bronwyn's dress, and Jacobs provided one of Landon's black cravats.

Knotting the two pieces of material together, Mr. Addair began the handfasting ceremony. "Greetings to one and all. We are here today to see Landon Neale, Earl of Hadfield, and Miss Bronwyn Cadby, join hands and be bound together by their love, now and forever."

Mr. Addair took Landon's left hand and Bronwyn's right as they stood side by side, facing the anvil. Interlocking their arms, Mr. Addair placed their palms flat together and began to wind the black and white material. First, about Landon's wrist and then around Bronwyn's, creating an intricate knotted design. Bronwyn was bound to him, as securely as the knot that connected their wrists. And unlike all the duties and responsibilities that bound him as PORF, this knot did not feel like restriction, but freedom.

Tucking the ends of the material, Mr. Addair patted their joined hands. "Do you, Landon Neale, take Bronwyn Cadby as wife?"

"I do."

Mr. Addair nodded, "Do you, Bronwyn Cadby, take his lordship, Landon Neale as husband?"

Landon held in a breath—turned and waited for Bronwyn's response.

Solemnly she answered, "I do."

Every muscle in his body relaxed. By Scottish law, they were wed. A declaration that they each wished to wed, in front of two witnesses, was all that was required. Originally, marrying and siring an heir had merely been another task to attend to. Rolling his eyes heavenward, he sent up a prayer of thanks for the precious gift he had received in Bronwyn. He committed to loving her for, however many days he had left. Cherishing and bedding her would be a blessing and not a burden.

Instead of dismissing everyone, Mr. Addair held out his hand, and his wife, who had stood slightly behind the man, placed two rings upon his palm. The innkeeper scanned the crowd. "These rings have no beginning and no end. Like the circle around us, each wedding band is an infinite thing—never changing yet always adaptable." He spoke in a clear voice that carried over the assembled audience. Mr. Addair slid a solid gold band onto Landon's ring finger. "True love itself is infinite. It knows no boundaries or restrictions."

Taking Bronwyn's left hand, Mr. Addair slid a thinner version of Landon's ring onto her ring finger. "Love flourishes and grows with time. Love cannot be forced and cannot be taken away. It is a gift you give to one another without demands."

Landon stared down at his wife. He'd caught a flicker of unease in her eyes as Mr. Addair finished his speech. The innkeeper had used the word love. While he was reasonably sure he was in love with Bronwyn, he had yet to say the words. Tonight, he'd tell her.

Peyton touched their bound hands. "My congratulations to you both."

Jacobs stepped forward next. "Best wishes, my lord, my lady."

Mr. Addair clapped his hands. "It is done. May I present to you all, the Earl and Countess of Hadfield."

A round of cheers came from the crowd. Bright smiles all around. They had come to witness the union of one of their own to a PORF, and none was more pleased than Landon himself.

CHAPTER ELEVEN

*C*ountess of Hadfield. Bronwyn pinched herself as she repeated her new identity. Instead of rollicking nerves and questions over what her future now entailed, Bronwyn's thoughts were solely focused on the consummation. Bound hand-in-hand to Landon, she entered the empty inn with Peyton and Jacobs behind them.

She nearly lost her balance as Landon came to a stop and turned to address the staff. "We won't be needing your services this eve." Her husband continued up the stairs to their chamber for the evening, leaving her no choice to follow. It also eliminated all chance of Peyton sharing any information she'd obtained on how Bronwyn should please Landon. Her bound hand began to sweat. How were they to have marital relations with their hands tied? She hated feeling unprepared. Their interludes in the coach had all centered around her pleasure. Even a ninny could deduce that there was more to the intimate act of consummating their marriage.

She turned slightly sideways to face Landon, in order to go up the narrow staircase. Her heart thudded harder against her ribs with each step they took.

Landon bent at the waist, causing her to hunch over too. Mirroring his movements invoked a sense of closeness. He slipped his free arm under her knees and lifted her, squeezing them through the tight doorway. In opposition to her natural tendency to seek out distance, Bronwyn straightened her back and wrapped her arm about his neck, bringing them even closer. Secure in his arms, Bronwyn rested her head against her husband's shoulder and closed her eyes. All her life, she had been bound by constraints to serve PORFs, and now she was one herself. While she didn't doubt that being a countess would have its own challenges, held in Landon's strong arms she found the freedom to simply be. None of her reactions to her husband were consistent.

Still cradling her in his arms, he sat on the bed. "I hope you don't mind. I didn't want to tread upon your toes, trying to enter through thw blasted door."

Uncertain of what was expected of her, Bronwyn remained quiet and waited. Her husband's tempting lips were curved into a lopsided grin. Resisting the desire to pull him closer and kiss him, she ran her free hand down over his shoulder and chest. Her breath hitched as his muscles flexed under her palm. Cursing the fine lawn fabric that separated them, she lowered her free hand to rest in her lap. The snow-white ribbon binding their hands caught her attention. Bound together. She was safe and secure, and oddly at peace with their union. But as Landon tugged at the loop of the material and untied the knots, her confidence unraveled. Fear filled the space between their hands, separating them anew.

Landon loosened the last knot. "You'll be free in a moment."

"I apologize for my sweaty hand."

"Oh, and here I believed mine was the sweaty one." His dimple appeared, and Bronwyn's heart melted.

She spied her wedding gift to him, lying upon the desk in the corner. Bronwyn had convinced Rutherford to create a pair of cuff links embossed with the letter "H" surrounded by laurel leaves. Old Man Rutherford had argued it would take him a week to create such pieces, but Bronwyn had wielded her power as Landon's wife-to-be, and the jeweler had acquiesced. At the time, a pang of guilt had her questioning her decision to employ the authority of a PORF when she had yet to officially become one.

As soon as her hand was freed from Landon's, she hopped off his lap and skipped over the desk, eager to see his reaction. She paused in front of two boxes of similar size—both with Rutherford's stamp upon the top and white ribbons securing the lid.

Bronwyn jumped as Landon's hand fell upon her shoulder. She frowned. "I'm not sure which one is my gift to you."

"Then let's both of us open them."

He reached around her, picked up the box on the left,

and placed it upon his palm. "You pull on this end, and I'll pull the other."

The ribbon fell away, and Bronwyn tentatively lifted the lid to reveal an exquisite charm bracelet. The bracelet itself was fashioned from silver and pearls. She lifted it out of the box to examine the charms. A horse. A falcon. A tiara. An angel and a harp. How very clever of him to select charms that represented both PORFs and the Network.

She glanced up to thank him, but his eyebrows had lifted with an element of surprise. "Is it not what you had ordered?"

Her husband cleared his throat. "It's perfect. But..." Landon sighed. Instead of continuing to speak he took the bracelet and opened the clasp.

She held out her wrist for him. The cold metal upon her skin raised goosebumps to her elbow. She waited for him to finish his sentence. Her breath caught in her throat as he brushed a finger along the inside of her wrist.

Landon inhaled deeply and then said, "It was not I who placed the order. Theo did on my behalf."

"It's still a thoughtful gift, no matter who gave Rutherford the order." She lifted her hand closer to inspect the charms.

"Theo always chooses the best gifts."

Had she heard correctly? Landon hadn't merely asked Theo to pass along the order. He had asked his cousin to select the wedding gift entirely. Her heart deflated.

She angled her face toward the floor to hide her

disappointment and reached for her gift to him. When she turned to give it to him, he lifted her chin, forcing her to meet his eyes.

"I'm sorry I've disappointed you. I should have selected your wedding gift myself, even if I made a hash of it."

She forced her lips to curl into a smile at his sincere apology. Logically she knew it impossible for a man like Landon to love her. He'd only had a few days to come to know the real her. She had opened up, wanting to make sure Landon was fully aware of who he'd be marrying once they crossed the border. Their time together had confirmed what a genuinely brilliant man Landon was and solidified her attraction to the rogue that lay beneath the surface.

Her smile transformed into a grin, and then Landon's lips were upon hers, banishing all thoughts and worries. She gave herself over to the man whose kisses awakened a feeling she never imagined possible.

Holding her tight, Landon asked, "May I have my gift now?"

She lifted her hand and held out the box for him.

Landon opened his gift, and his dimples appeared in full force. "Now, these are a thoughtful gift. I shall treasure them forever." He placed them back on the desk. "How can I atone for my mistake?"

"You could kiss me again."

Her husband didn't hesitate. He gathered her back into his arms. His fingers ran along the seam of buttons at her back as his lips glided over hers, hungry with desire.

Gasping for air, Landon twirled her around. He made quick work of removing her gown and stays. Standing in her chemise, stockings, and slippers, she stared at the bed. Anticipation crept up her spine and her stomach did a flip. This beautiful, brilliant man was to be hers in every way. Certainty that she was going to fail him refused to leave her.

It had always worked to her advantage when she took matters into her own hands. She grabbed Landon by the hand and led him to the bed. At her gentle push, he fell back and sat upon the straw-stuffed mattress.

Before he could question her, she placed her hands on her hips and said, "I've decided upon a different punishment." She nearly laughed out loud as his eyes enlarged to the size of saucers.

His Adam's apple bobbed up and down. "I'm ready for my sentence."

"For the remainder of the evening, you will be required to *tell me* your preferences and dislikes—in words, not via sounds or movements." She lifted the hem of her chemise up and over her head.

Landon's gaze affixed to her breasts.

She bent to remove her garters, stockings, and shoes. Bronwyn rose until they were eye to eye. "Do you understand?"

"I believe so."

Naked, she stepped between his legs. Steadying her hands, she removed his cravat and said, "Good."

Landon licked his lips, and Bronwyn's fingers faltered as she worked on the buttons of his waistcoat.

Her husband didn't appear at all perturbed at her bold actions. His responses merely empowered Bronwyn to continue with her brazen acts. At the same time, she was powerless over the intense craving to have him touch and pleasure her.

Landon's hands wrapped around her hips, and he tugged Bronwyn closer. Her skin burned as warm breath brushed against her breasts. "I'd prefer you undressed me quicker." Desire and desperation that matched her own rang clear in his voice. His lips skimmed over her nipples, eliciting a moan from her.

Taking a half step back, Bronwyn said, "Very well. Stand."

Landon released his hold on her, but not before running his hands over her bottom and giving her a little swat. The brief sting sent a thrill of excitement through her that clenched the inner muscles at her center.

He toed off his court shoes and slowly stood, feet braced apart. Her breathing and pulse both accelerated as she divested him of his coat, waistcoat, and lawn shirt. When she reached for his falls, he captured her wrist. "I was wrong." His voice was raw and deep. "I'd prefer you to take your time."

His words ignited a war within her. For days, Bronwyn had been curious as to what his manhood would feel like in her hand. Her fingers trembled as she reached for his falls. The need to please him superseded her own cravings. The material of Landon's breeches was stretched taut, easing slightly as she released each button through its hole. His shaft sprang free and grazed the back of her hand. Wrapping her fingers about his member, she slid her palm down until she could run her thumb over the tip.

"Perhaps you...you could continue your exploration." Landon's breathing became erratic. "Once I'm upon the bed." He released a groan as he grew in her grip. "I fear my knees might buckle."

Glad it wasn't only she who felt weak when caressed, Bronwyn slipped her hands beneath his waistband at his hips and shimmied his breeches down until they dropped to the floor. Dropping to her knees, she rolled down his stockings. He lifted each foot, allowing her to remove them from his big feet.

His hard shaft bobbed once as she drew level with it. Steadying herself, she placed her hands upon his muscled upper thighs, stuck out her tongue, and licked. Finding the taste not unpleasant, she ran the tip of him along the seam of her lips.

Landon's fingers threaded through her hair, and with a little pressure, pressed himself against her mouth. Instinctively she opened, and she slid her lips down his member, which twitched. Her hands roamed to the sides of his taut thighs up to his hips and then back round to his tightly clenched butt cheeks. The man had dimples. Imitating his earlier actions, Bronwyn ran her hand over his ass and gave it a slap. His grip tightened in her hair. Her moan mixed with his. A second groan of pure pleasure escaped her husband as she tightened her lips about him. Bronwyn inched back to the tip. With a pop, she released him. "You're not using your words."

"Wife. You may take me in your mouth any time you like."

"Would you like for me to now?"

"If you wish, but I believe I stated my preference to be abed."

Her gaze darted between the bed behind him and his hard shaft. Bracing against his muscular thighs, she slowly rose, brushing her nipples against him as she stood.

Landon growled, "If I'm to consummate our marriage, you had best get into bed."

Scrambling under the covers, Bronwyn settled herself on her back.

Landon slid next to her and placed his hands behind his head. "Would you like to continue your exploration, or may I conduct my own?"

Hmm. What a dilemma. "What would you prefer?" Bronwyn asked.

"In this instance, I have no preference and will defer to your wishes." Landon rolled on to his side and stared, waiting for her decision.

"May I touch you if you are the one conducting the expedition?"

"Certainly."

"Then I wish for you to lead."

Landon's hand cupped her face. Her breath hitched as he leaned forward to run his tongue along her bottom lip. Her skin pricked as her husband's broad hand traveled down her neck. She pressed her aching breast into the palm of his hand and then placed her own hand over his. Bronwyn squeezed, causing his fingers to pinch her nipple the way that sent sparks throughout her body. She rolled onto her side to get closer, but Landon pushed her flat on her back. Peppering kisses down her neck, over the swell of her breast, Landon removed his hand and circled her nipple with his tongue. Hedonistic and delightful shocks of pleasure ran down to her core. He obliviated her fear of the unknown and of new experiences and replaced it with yearning. Bronwyn pressed Landon's head to her just as he had pressed himself to her earlier.

He grazed his teeth against her nipple and suckled until she writhed against the bed. Releasing her breast, he moved on to the other, repeating his torturous movements.

Bronwyn silently called out his name, but only moans of pleasure escaped her throat.

Landon shifted closer. "Spread your legs." Settling himself between her thighs, he loomed over her and whispered in her ear. "I've waited four long days. Wanting to bury myself deep inside you." His declaration disproved her brother's claims she'd never attract a man with her boyish interests and behavior.

On a ragged breath, Landon said, "I prefer to linger. But tonight, I can't wait." He trailed kisses along her jaw. "I promise next time..." He grabbed his member and guided it over her neither lips, before gently pushing at her entrance. "Later, we can both explore."

She wiggled, unsure if she wanted more of him or to squirm away. When he stilled, she did too. His features were strained.

"Is something the matter?" Bronwyn asked.

He let his head fall to her shoulder. "I don't want to hurt you. I can't."

She had heard whispers that some women found marital relations painful or unpleasant, but every one of Landon's touches brought her pleasure. "I've not experienced any discomfort."

Landon moved to roll onto his back.

The loss of pressure between her legs made her ache with an intensity that bordered on pain.

She grabbed his hand and placed it against her core. "I need you..."

His fingers curled and entered her, relieving some of her need, but it wasn't enough.

She moved to straddle him. Hovering above his shaft, uncertain of exactly how to proceed, she said, "I want you inside of me, not your fingers."

He grabbed his member and like before, he rubbed it against her as she slowly pressed down, lowering herself inch by inch. His thumb circled the sensitive nub that sent heated waves of excitement through her. She was nearly fully seated upon him when a sharp sting made her flinch and close her eyes. Her legs collapsed, causing her to sink all the way to his base.

His groan opened her eyes. "Was that the pain you wished not to cause me?"

"Aye." He shifted, and the movement sent pleasure shooting up her spine. Oddly, her nipples became sensitive.

Her breasts ached. She reached for his hands, guiding

them over her sides and up to cup the sensitive globes. Landon kneaded the tender flesh. The urge to move was impossible to ignore. Her husband's small movements urged her to rock back and forth. Uncertain how to alleviate the mounting need within her, she set a tentative pace. Landon lowered his hand to her hips, and Bronwyn increased the pace of her actions. His fingers dug into her backside as he assisted her in raising slightly. Bronwyn sank back down and circled her hips. His hands roamed back up to her breasts. Bronwyn rose and lowered herself, slowly at first and then faster and with more vigor as Landon's groans became more profound and louder. Proud she was able to please her husband, Bronwyn increased her efforts.

Landon pinched her nipples hard, and an upsurge of pleasure rolled through her, sending her over the crest of the wave. She collapsed against her husband's chest as he continued to pump himself into her over and over. His fingers bit into her hips, he let out one long moan, and then he slowed his movements.

Landon stroked her back up and down along her spine. "Next time, I promise it will be better."

How could it be better? Would she able to endure more?

She wasn't certain. Her brain was incapable of working at that moment, and her body was limp. Sleepily she mumbled, "Goodnight, husband."

"Rest while I recover."

Landon's response was confusing. But being a good wife, she obeyed her husband and closed her eyes.

CHAPTER TWELVE

A master at feigning sleep, Bronwyn shimmied closer to the edge of the bed. Her worries over whether her husband would wish to repeat the marital act were all for naught. Landon had kept her awake practically all night. His mere touch wreaked havoc with her pulse and denied her brain the oxygen it needed to think. On the rare occasion she found herself awake while Landon slept, her husband had an odd habit of mumbling in his sleep. At first, she believed Landon's sleep talk was merely words jumbled up, but then she realized they were anastrophes. To her utter surprise, most were about love—love for her. Bronwyn's favorite of the night was "Oxymoron, you told me I was. Love before never like this." She had forgotten the details of their first argument, but she clearly recalled referring to him as an oxymoron. At the time, she had believed him to be a kind dictator, not the charming rogue she had married.

Landon's arm wrapped about her waist and pulled

her closer. "Good morn, wife."

Apparently, her husband was a light sleeper. She'd have to remember that, for she needed time to muddle through Landon's confessions of having loved her long before he proposed.

Warm lips pressed against her neck. Landon mumbled, "I'll confess, I failed to consider what was to occur after we were wed."

"Even without a strategy, I believe you performed magnificently."

He placed kisses upon her bare shoulder. "I wasn't referring to right after the ceremony. I meant I've made no arrangements for today."

Bronwyn turned to face her husband. "Absolutely no plans?"

Sheepishly Landon said, "Well, there are a few matters I must attend to, but none that I shouldn't be able to deal with swiftly. Do you wish to travel abroad? I can make the necessary arrangements posthaste."

Traveling to the Continent was the last thing she wished for. She'd never had the opportunity to learn a second language. Mastering English without a cockney accent had taken her months; it would take just as many for her to learn French. She would never presume that everyone she would interact with would understand or speak English.

Bronwyn sighed. "I'm ill-prepared to venture to a foreign country, although I'm fully prepared to learn whatever languages are necessary...if you don't mind hiring me a tutor."

"Why would I mind?" Landon kissed her nose. "But if you wish to go, I'd be more than happy to act as your translator."

She didn't want to be a burden to him. No. Truthfully, she didn't want to rely on him. Resting her forehead on Landon's chest, Bronwyn said, "Plus, there are other things I still need to educate myself on."

"Such as?" Landon tugged at the ends of her hair that rested in the middle of her back.

She raised her head. "How to become a proper lady. How to run a household. How to..."

Landon's lips crushed hers. She pulled back and said, "You didn't let me finish. I was about to say how to satisfy my husband's needs."

"My needs?" Landon's dimple appeared as he chuckled. "The staff and the innkeeper will want to know about our plans." Landon cupped her face. "And I'm prepared to prove to you again if necessary that you are quite capable of meeting my every desire."

Bronwyn frowned. "I wasn't referring to *those* needs."

Landon smoothed her brow with his thumb and wiggled his eyebrows at her.

Grinning, Bronwyn tried to redirect her husband's wayward thoughts. "What would be your preference?"

"I'm quite happy to defer to your wishes on the matter."

She'd expected him to be in a rush to return to London. Bronwyn knew many sought out his wisdom on various matters. For their entire journey to Scotland, he had given her his complete focus. Guilt at having occupied all his time spurred her answer. "I wish to return to London."

His eyes brightened as he asked, "Are you certain?"

She had already taken up too much of his time. "Yes, quite."

"Then it's decided." With a hand on her bottom, he pressed her closer. His arousal slid between her legs. "But first, it might be prudent on my part to prove again how certain I am that you are more than capable of meeting my every need. Shall we delay our departure until later in the day?"

Bronwyn moaned as he rotated his hips in a circular motion. She closed her eyes and said, "As you wish."

LANDON PEERED up from the stack of correspondence he'd diligently worked on since they entered the traveling coach. His teasing gaze lowered to her chest and then wandered back up to meet her eyes. Her cheeks flushed, but she remained silent. She glanced down at his impressive penmanship—neat and precise as if he had written his responses at his old desk at the offices of Neale & Sons and not jostled about traveling along a Scottish road. Having departed late in the day, they wouldn't make it far before having to stop. Bronwyn crossed her arms and pushed the swell of her bosom up. Her nipples threatened to peek out from her décolleté. "Will we be traveling past dusk?"

Landon folded up his traveling desk and hastily

placed it on the seat next to him. He slid over to sit next to her. "No. I'd not dare take the risk and place you in danger."

Bronwyn frowned and turned to face her husband. The Network had inns strategically placed within a solid day's travel of each other. "But the next suitable inn is at least another half day's travel."

"Lord and Countess Waterford reside not far from here. They will be delighted to host us for a night."

Landon dipped his head, and she leaned in to meet his lips. The man created an insatiable need within her. Hiking up her skirts, she straddled him.

Settled upon his lap, she cupped his face and said, "Lord Waterford's family is the only one within the Network to have served PORFs longer than mine. I'm told his wife is the daughter of a duke and possesses unusual talents."

"Lady Mary is an angel."

The admiration in her husband's tone set her blood to boil. Sorry she had mentioned the lady's name, Bronwyn set out to banish Lady Mary from Landon's mind. She lowered her mouth to kiss him, and in doing so, her gown slid lower, displaying her pert nipples. Landon cupped her breast and rolled her tender nipples between his forefinger and thumb while his tongue invaded her mouth. A low moan escaped her throat as his left hand ran along the back of her calf and then rested on the top of her thigh.

Bronwyn pulled back and gasped for air. "I'm nervous about meeting the couple. What if they..."

"There is no need to be worried. They will adore you as I do." Landon gave her a hard-searing kiss. "As wife to the PORF who possesses the rondure, they have pledged their loyalty and allegiance to you."

That was the problem. Going forward, many would treat her with respect and reverence merely due to the fact she was Landon's wife, and not because she had earned their regard.

The horses' hooves slowed to a walk, and the crunch of pebbles beneath the wheels indicated they had turned off the dirt path and onto Waterford's estate. Bronwyn scrambled off Landon's lap and fell back onto his traveling desk. Sliding to the seat, she adjusted her dress and was smoothing out her skirts as the coach came to a halt. The door swung open. Landon exited and turned to assist her.

Landon took her hand and said, "Waterford can be a burr, but I'm certain you will find Lady Mary to be most kind and generous."

On the portico, the entire staff was lined up to greet them. Where were Lord Waterford and his wife? The butler stepped forward. A sealed parchment lay in the center of a silver tray, which he presented to Landon.

Her husband said, "Duncan. Where are Waterford and Mary?"

Bronwyn was no expert in etiquette, but even she knew Landon should have addressed the lady of the house by her title, not by her given name. Such familiarity was usually reserved for family members. Whatever relationship Landon had developed with Lady

Mary, it had blossomed quickly, for he hadn't even been acquainted with her prior to his inheriting the earldom. The Network had kept an eye on the woman for years since Waterford, a council elder, was betrothed to the blasted lady.

The butler replied, "Countess Waterford instructed me that all will be explained." He nodded to the missive.

Was it a love note? Her heart raced once again as Landon retrieved the letter. He shifted to allow her to read it with him.

Landon -
Since you failed to make the appropriate arrange-
ments, I have taken it upon myself to prepare
them for you.
Waterford and I will be residing with Aunt Agnes
for a fortnight.
We will not be far should you need our assistance.

Countess of Hadfield –
Our congratulations. I sincerely hope to make
your acquaintance before you depart.
In the meantime, the staff are at your disposal;
however, if you should have any issues, advise
Duncan to send for me.
Best wishes
Mary

Not a love note.

In fact, Lady Mary's tone was rather forward, given she was addressing the most senior-ranking PORF.

Landon chucked as he refolded the parchment. "Lady Mary may take credit, but I'd wager it was Lady Frances's doing."

"Who is Lady Frances?"

"A close companion and advisor to Lady Mary."

"Does she reside with them? Will I meet her?"

"Hmm... Yes, she does reside with them, but no one—not even Waterford—has technically had the pleasure of meeting the extremely wise and meddling Lady Frances."

Bronwyn's knowledge of Lady Mary was limited to a few facts. Daughter of a duke. Her brother closest in age and Waterford's best friend had died upon the battle-field. She recently brought Waterford up to snuff and married him. And, ah, yes...the rumors. "It's true? Lady Mary can see and talk to the dead?"

Landon needn't answer. The stiffening of the staff's posture told Bronwyn they did not care for her shocking statement regarding their mistress.

Landon took her elbow and guided her to the front door. "Yes, Mary has the gift."

"Oh, I've never met anyone with such a talent. I'm ever so glad Lady Mary invited us to stay. I do wish to meet her."

From behind, Duncan mumbled, "Be careful what ye wish for."

CHAPTER THIRTEEN

*B*ed linens tangled about his legs, Landon stretched out and wiggled until his feet came free. Three days, he'd laid about with his beguiling wife— three long nights of pleasuring her until they fell asleep with exhaustion. Bronwyn was eager to please him in and out of bed. He had shared the tale of how he came to be in possession of the rondure, and she shared the details of cases she and Christopher had dealt with since his departure from the firm.

In all the hours they spent together, he hadn't managed to find an appropriate time to confess his love for her. The woman excelled at directing and redirecting conversations. Not once had she indicated she might return his regard. While they were indisputably compatible in bed, he believed it had the potential to be much more. The one element missing was love. But as time passed, Landon became increasingly wary. The fear of her not returning the words of endearment caused him to postpone sharing his deepest feelings for her.

Bronwyn twisted to look over her shoulder at him. "I'd like to explore the castle and the grounds today."

"That sounds like a wonderful idea."

"Don't you have other matters to attend to? I'm sure there is a stack of correspondence somewhere that needs your attention."

"Have you tired of my company already?" His question got her full attention.

She turned and to face him. "I'd happily lie abed with you all day, but I am aware that you have been neglecting your duties. I can't bear the guilt of occupying all your time any longer."

"Is that what has been bothering you?"

She stared at him hard. "Aren't you bored of my company?"

"Definitely not." Unable to resist, he placed a chaste kiss upon her lips.

"Really. Most people tire of my constant debating after an hour or less."

"Your ability to systematically point out the flaws of any argument is one of the things I adore about you."

Her cheeks turned a pretty rose color. "In any case, I know what it is like to be the one waiting for a decision on a matter to be made. Attend to your responsibilities, and I shall go on an adventure."

If they tackled the mountain of letters awaiting him together, the sooner he could return to more pleasurable pursuits with his wife. "Would you like to assist me?"

"Are you certain you want my help?"

"It would be like before, at the firm."

A smirk appeared on Bronwyn's otherwise serious features. "My thanks for the offer, but I think the sunshine will do me good."

Odd. Landon had been confident Bronwyn would leap at the opportunity. Instead, his wife placed a kiss upon his forehead and disappeared into the adjoining chamber.

With impeccable timing, Jacobs appeared in the doorway with a lawn shirt at the ready. Stepping into his breeches, Landon fastened his falls and padded over to the door. "What is it, Jacobs?"

"A missive from your brother arrived this morn."

Landon punched his arms into the shirtsleeves. Whatever the matter was, it must be of import, for Christopher was fully aware that Archbroke was in charge until his return.

BRONWYN STEPPED in front of the large looking glass as she wrapped the lovely tartan Lady Mary had left as a wedding gift for her about her shoulders. The prickle of the fine wool against her skin reminded Bronwyn that this was to be her new life. Glorious gowns made from expensive silks and material, staff to wait upon her every need, and meals that burst with flavors she'd not thought possible. This was the life of a lady, not one she'd ever envisioned for herself. Hadn't her parents always warned: *Never forget your station in life. Best to keep your head on straight. Be happy with your lot.* Like a good and dutiful daughter, she'd never debated her parents' thinking.

She narrowed her gaze at the woman staring back at her. How had Landon described her eyes? A shade of aquamarine with shards of sparkling sunlight. No, the man was wrong. Her eyes were a dull shade of sky blue. She reached up to place a wayward wisp of her mouse-brown hair behind her ear. It was definitely not the vibrant, varied chestnut-brown color Landon had proclaimed it. Turning away in disgust, she regained her senses. She was no beauty, but when Landon's intense gaze landed upon her, she felt like a diamond of the first water. Landon was a rogue in disguise, constantly feeding her mind with crazy images of herself. Nightly she pondered the question that continued to plague her. Why her? Why had Landon deemed her worthy over the elegant ladies of the ton or any other woman of his acquaintance? She was no extraordinary beauty. She wasn't any more intelligent than Emma or any of the other women in the Network, and she certainly wasn't as brilliant or as brave as Theo. Bronwyn glanced back in the looking glass and shook her head.

She scanned the bedchamber for her husband. Her eyes fixed upon the rumpled bed linens—why had she even suggested leaving the bed today?

Gripping the tartan at the center of her chest, she sighed. Guilt. She couldn't go on pretending. Landon's nightly confessions of his love for her and mumblings of worry at having abandoned his responsibilities weighed heavily upon her chest.

Tip-toeing down the hall, she slinked out the front door and escaped into the fresh air. *That was easier than expected.* The slew of carefully crafted arguments to escape the castle unaccompanied went unused. Not a single day had passed since Landon's proposal that she had managed to venture out of doors without a team of footmen trailing her.

With her face tilted sunwards, Bronwyn basked in its warmth. She loosened her tight hold on her shawl, relaxing the muscles in her shoulders. A good brisk walk would help her clear her cloudy thoughts. Stopped, at a fork in the path, Landon's suggestion to assist him like before replayed in her mind. How could he even suggest a thing?

Much had changed. Two years had passed.

He had changed. Landon was no longer solely focused on his occupation as a barrister, happily unaware of his family's ties to the Crown, and unmarked. He was a peer with unparalleled duties to the Crown and the Network.

She had changed. No longer merely a shopkeeper's daughter. She was a valued legal assistant and reveled in working in the legal offices of Neale & Sons.

Bronwyn kicked a small pebble over and over, punctuating each thought until it disappeared into the long grass. Walking aimlessly, she ventured into the woods and mulled over her new circumstance. Years of studying legal matters alongside Landon, and then

Christopher, were no longer of value. She lacked the knowledge to run a successful household—meal planning, selection of décor, which charities to support. Frustrated, Bronwyn increased her pace. She would be expected to hire and train servants. People who were once her friends would become members of her household staff. She was no better than any of them. No more important.

Bronwyn clutched her shawl tighter. The heat of the sun fled as she continued deeper into the woods. Tall, broad trees cast dark shadows that mirrored her mood.

Landon alluded to his need for a partner. Her mum and dad were partners. Her mum had assisted her dad in running the store while she carried and raised five children. And her dad made no qualms about declaring he'd be lost without her mum's assistance. Bronwyn's shoulders sagged. Would Landon ever be able to make such a claim?

Increasing her pace, she stomped farther into the woods. With each step, Bronwyn's resolve deepened—one way or another, she was going to aid Landon. *But how?*

A tree limb hidden beneath fallen leaves caught her foot, toppling Bronwyn onto her knees. Rolling to her side, she brushed the crumpled leaves from her injured ankle and gingerly pressed around the joint. No broken bones, but it was tender to the touch and beginning to swell. Through the tree branches, the sun was barely visible. With her injury, it would take her twice as long to return to the castle. Holding her breath, she placed her foot flat upon the ground and tried to stand. Shooting pain caused her to fall back on to her bottom. *Blast!*

Bronwyn searched the ground for a stick thick enough to provide support. Luck was not on her side today. Nothing but small twigs and dry leaves lay on the trail floor. Born and raised in town, she'd imagined the woods peaceful, but now they were eerily quiet. She was all alone and absolutely out of her element. Heaving in deep breaths, she calmed her mind.

The crunch of boots behind her sent her scrambling on her knees.

Red leather slippers appeared before her. "Lady Bronwyn. May I be of assistance?"

The woman wore skirts of sturdy blue velvet. A tartan comprised of forest green and dark navy squares separated by bright yellow yarn was draped across one of the lady's shoulders and around her waist. The material mirrored the design of Bronwyn's shawl. She must be at the feet of her hostess—Lady Mary, the Countess of Waterford.

Bronwyn raised her gaze inch by inch until the warmth of Lady Mary's friendly smile called forth an answering grin. It was no wonder Landon spoke of Lady Mary with awe. She was a gorgeous woman.

Lady Mary crouched down. "Would you prefer Gilbert carry you back?"

Barely above a whisper, Bronwyn asked, "How did you find me?"

"Aunt Agnes lives a good two hours' ride from here. We set out when I was informed you were lost. They made no mention of you being hurt. I apologize for not arriving sooner; we had a tad bit of trouble locating you."

"Why didn't they advise you of my location?"

Lady Mary frowned. "My sources aggravatingly only share what they believe is pertinent."

Bronwyn couldn't help but laugh at Lady Mary's response and exasperated look. She swallowed the last half of a laugh as a tall, athletically built man came into sight. "I'd like to try and walk on my own and not be carried like a babe."

Placing a hand on the man's arm for leverage, Lady Mary rose. "Can you assist Lady Bronwyn to her feet?"

"Certainly. Countess Hadfield, please allow me to assist." He bent and placed an arm about her waist. "Place your arm along my shoulders, behind my neck."

In one swift motion, he lifted her to stand, but the pain in her ankle had her grimacing. One quick side glance at her, and Lord Waterford bent, placed an arm under her knees, and lifted her.

Lady Mary picked up Bronwyn's tartan and brushed off the leaves clinging to it. Placing the material about Bronwyn's shoulders, Lady Mary said, "We will have you safely home soon, and it will be bed rest for you for a few days."

Days! Bronwyn shook her head. Landon's sleepy mumbling of guilt at having left Archbroke with an enormous burden filled her mind. "I'm certain I'll be fine by morn," Bronwyn declared. "I'll not be a burden to Landon." A wife was to assist and aid her husband, not become a hindrance.

The couple glanced at each other with a manner that suggested an entire conversation had occurred between the two in mere seconds.

Lord Waterford smiled down at her. "Lassie, you're no' a burden to anyone."

In a matter of fact tone, Lady Mary said, "Landon won't let you out of his sight once he sees you've been hurt."

"Then *you* will assist me in ensuring he doesn't find out."

Eyebrows raised, Lady Mary asked, "Is that an order, Countess Hadfield?"

Was her first order going to be one to deceive her husband?

Bronwyn nodded.

"Very well. So be it." Mary grinned. "Gilbert, you will carry Lady Bronwyn into the castle and ensure she is settled in the drawing room. I'll distract Landon."

Bronwyn had a sinking feeling that she had made an enormous error.

CHAPTER FOURTEEN

Seated at Waterford's monstrosity of a desk, Landon traced a finger over the boyishly formed letters. G. E. T. He pictured a younger version of his friend Gilbert Elliot Talbot carving his initials into the tabletop. An ornate silver candlestick holder sat to the right of the markings. Landon picked up his quill to complete his response to Christopher's inquiry as to when he and Bronwyn would be returning to town. But the words he should be penning were not in alignment with his wishes. For the first time in his life, he wanted to ignore his responsibilities and lay abed all day with his wife. A glint of sunlight reflected off the silver candleholder. It was situated in the most unlikely of spots to provide adequate lighting. He picked up the candleholder and revealed freshly carved initials: MEMT. Mary Eloise Masterson Talbot. Setting the candleholder back down off to the side, he traced the letters marked into the wood. Was Waterford as bewitched with his wife as Landon found himself with his?

At the fall of heavy, booted footsteps and the patter of slippers from the hall, Landon shoved the candleholder back to its original spot. The door swished open. Mary strode in, came to an abrupt halt inches shy of the desk, and planted her hands on her hips. "Why didn't you ensure that your wife had an escort while wandering about the estate?"

Landon put quill to paper and scribbled a hasty reply to Christopher. He signed his name, leaned back, and steepled his fingers beneath his chin.

Mary glared at him as she stood in front of the desk. "Well?"

Landon peered around Mary. "Where is your husband?"

"About." Mary waved her hand dismissively and then replaced it upon her hip. "You will not be rid of me until I have an answer."

He wanted to be in his wife's company. He missed her. Although anxious to see Bronwyn again, he'd have to deal with Mary first. He arched a brow and said, "What would you do if Waterford commanded a retinue follow you about morn, noon and night?"

The woman's shoulders sagged. "I'd tell him he was ridiculously overprotective."

"Not that I need to explain or justify my actions to you, but the grounds are patrolled. There have been no reported threats since we arrived. Besides, I sensed

Bronwyn wished for a bit of time to herself. Thus, I gave the order to give her a wide berth. Why are you here?"

"I was advised I was needed here."

"Really?"

"Yes. I believe it best if I left the explanations to your wife."

Was Bronwyn that upset?

Landon sat forward. "Did she send for you?"

"Not in the typical fashion."

Landon stood, and Mary averted her gaze.

He considered whether or not to press her for more information. Had Mary's sources insinuated that Bronwyn was unhappy? Did Bronwyn regret marrying him? Afraid of the answers, Landon turned and strode to the door. He stood to the side and waited for Mary to join him, but she remained unmoving.

"Shall we join our spouses? I assume they are waiting for us in the drawing room."

"Aren't you going to subject me to one of your cross-examinations?"

"Did you not suggest I seek the answers directly from Bronwyn?"

Mary sighed and proceeded to walk toward him. "I did." Stopping inches from him, she turned and said, "She has yet to realize how important she is to you and the Network."

As usual, Mary spoke the truth. He shouldn't have assumed Bronwyn understood the value she could provide, having an intimate knowledge of the inner workings of the Network, but most importantly, he had failed to tell her he loved her.

Mary entered the hallway and was approached by Duncan, who bent to whisper in his mistress's ear.

"Thank you for the update." Mary faced Landon and said, "Bronwyn has twisted her ankle. Duncan assures me no broken bones, but a few days of rest will be required."

His wife was hurt. Blood drained from his face.

Running to the drawing-room, he rushed to Bronwyn's side. He crouched down to take a look at her injury. "Love, how did this happen?"

Mary slapped his hand away from his wife's ankle. "Stop fawning over her in front of company." Landon didn't miss the mischievous grin Mary gave her husband as she added, "You are behaving like a besotted fool."

Ignoring his host, he carefully touched Bronwyn's bandaged foot. "Does it hurt?"

"Not at all. Lord Waterford did a splendid job of wrapping it." Bronwyn removed her foot from his grasp and laid it back upon a tall pile of pillows.

He peered over at Waterford. Something was amiss. If Mary had only learned of the mishap, how had Waterford attended to her injury so swiftly?

"Lady Mary advised me that you have somehow inadvertently summoned her home. What is the matter in which you need Mary's aid and not mine?"

Bronwyn sat up straighter. "You, husband, are not a lady. I require etiquette lessons before I return to

London. I do not wish to embarrass you in front of your friends and peers."

As her words sank in, his heart soared with hope. His wife had not only asked for assistance, but she had also finally voiced one of the fears he had suspected lurked behind her original refusal to marry him. He'd not deny her request and set their progress back. He loved the bold, wonderful woman who was glowering at him. Landon smiled.

"Oh, don't try to distract me with that dimple of yours. I'm serious." Bronwyn raised her chin.

Her eyes never left his. *This* was the woman he had fantasized about for two years. Brazen, matter of fact, and logical—absolutely magnificent—proving his belief Bronwyn was the ideal woman for him.

Mary came to stand next to him. "Countess Hadfield, it would be my honor to assist you in any manner you request."

"Please, call me Bronwyn."

"Absolutely not." Mary shook her head and grinned at his bewildered wife.

Mary was a wily one.

Landon's gaze darted between the two women, who continued to glare at one another. Bronwyn's initial shock was gone, and Mary's smile had a devilish quality he'd not seen before. He had anticipated the two women would get along like kindred spirits, but there they were, engaged in what appeared to be a battle of wills much like his own with Bronwyn. Who would break the silence first? While he was curious to find out, a distinct chill had descended upon the room. Landon coughed to clear his throat. He turned to Waterford and said, "Let's adjourn to the study."

Waterford exited the room without a word; the man needed no further encouragement to leave. As Landon crossed the threshold, he glanced over his shoulder. He trusted Mary's judgment, but without knowledge of her plan, he worried his wife might not survive the cutting wit Mary could employ if she desired.

He caught up to Waterford in the hall. "Did you not find our wives' behavior odd?"

"Mary? Odd? Never." Waterford scoffed.

"Who do you think will win the war?"

Duncan appeared with a silver coin balanced on the tip of his thumb. The butler flipped the shilling into the air. "Heads it will be my mistress, tails Countess Hadfield."

Landon caught the coin midair. "Do you truly believe it a coin toss?"

"Lady Mary may be a duke's daughter and highly regarded amongst your set, but Lady Bronwyn has always been regarded as a leader among us. You have merely made it official."

"My hope is Bronwyn will come to view herself as you and I do."

"While my mistress has only been introduced to the workings of the Network for a year, Lady Mary is a quick study, remarkably kind and sage. Her methods may be unorthodox, but if anyone can instruct your wife on how best to handle the sharp claws and harsh gossip of the ton, it will be Lady Mary."

Landon opened his palm to reveal the coin. Tails. Was that a good or a bad sign?

BRONWYN BROKE down first and asked, "Would you care to explain why you will not address me by my given name?"

"I'd be honored to." Mary sank into the chair opposite to Bronwyn. "I shall be more than happy to address you as you wish just as soon as you can refrain from making that awful, shrewish face whenever someone addresses you by the title and station you hold."

"That's ridiculous. I never make faces."

"Oh, but you do. Until you can master plastering an all-too-sweet smile upon your pretty features in any situation, I shall address you as Countess Hadfield."

Bronwyn attempted to school her features into her best angelic impression. "Ugh. What if I gave you an order not to?"

"I shall have to suffer the consequences." Mary winked at Bronwyn and then moved to sit next to her on the settee. "You say you want to learn how to go about in society. But I say there is no need. You should be true to yourself." Her hostess grabbed her hand in a friendly gesture and squeezed her hand. "Landon doesn't care a fig about the opinions of the ton. He cares about his duties to the Crown and the safety of those within the

Network. Landon is no fool. He chose you, and for a good reason."

"Not for love." The words had tumbled out of Bronwyn's mouth before she even gave it thought.

Mary waved a hand wildly in the air. "Bah. He loves you even if he hasn't said the words. Men are slow to confess." Mary patted her hand. "Have you fallen in love with him?"

"I fell in love with him when he was a barrister." Like moments before, she had spoken without thought or hesitation. Mary wasn't like the other society ladies who had meekly followed their husbands into the office of Neale & Sons. Bronwyn confided, "I'm not sure I can be the wife Landon needs me to be now that he is...."

"You are the head PORF's wife. The members of the Network will seek your approval, not the other way around. As the Countess of Hadfield, you shall receive invitations to the most sought-after events, routs, musicales, balls, garden parties..." Mary paused to inhale. "Card parties, water parties, soirees...you understand. However, I anticipate before long you will be the one setting trends much like the Duchess of Fairmont."

"She's a duchess. I'm a shopkeeper's daughter who masqueraded as a legal assistant."

"Lady Dorinda wasn't always a duchess. But the woman wields her power with such grace one would never believe she hadn't been born and raised to rule."

"How does she do it?"

"Countess Hadfield."

Bronwyn relaxed every muscle in her forehead.

Mary continued, "It matters not how Lady Dorinda manages. It only matters how *you* shall tackle the responsibilities of your position."

"Well, I'm glad I have you to assist me."

"I hope you will still be of the same mind tomorrow."

CHAPTER FIFTEEN

*F*ingers interlocked and head cradled in his hands, Landon stared up at the ceiling. If Mary was successful in her lessons, he'd end up with a wife he had no interest in. Meek, obedient, docile—those were definitely not the traits he wished Bronwyn to exhibit. His wife's bold fiery nature was one of her greatest assets. And if he wanted obedience, he'd purchase a hound, not expect it of his wife.

Mary was welcomed into the most elite circles, and Landon didn't question Mary's knowledge on the subject. However, he couldn't recall a time when Mary herself had heeded all the ridiculous rules she'd imparted during her etiquette lessons with Bronwyn.

Each night Bronwyn returned to their chambers in a state of pure flummox. His wife would stand at the end of the bed, hands on her hips, and in her best imitation of Mary, recite the day's lesson. Landon would listen to the preposterous rule and then proceed to expel the horrid concept from her mind. He had learned the first evening that simply informing his wife to ignore the crazed lessons would not work. Bronwyn had insisted she must master these lessons. So each night, he resolved to teach her why it was essential not to abide by the strictures, especially in bed. Yesterday's lesson that a lady should defer to her husband in all matters had required an extraordinary amount of patience on his part to exorcise the ideal. Finally, with the first streaks of light coming in through the thick window coverings, Bronwyn had taken command of their lovemaking and rode him hard until she found her pleasure.

Landon hugged his exhausted wife's limp form close. She was magnificent. But what he loved most was her sharp mind and unwavering determination. How was he to explain to her that these rules did not apply to her?

He had two options, put a cease to the lessons or instruct Mary to teach Bronwyn how to best navigate around the rules. Landon grinned as he ran his fingers through his wife's hair. Mary was a master at circumventing the rules. He'd see to it that Mary assisted Bronwyn to do the same, but one couldn't evade a rule if one didn't know it existed. He finally saw the wisdom in Bronwyn's insistence in learning all the blasted guidelines a lady should follow in the name of good manners.

Bronwyn's sleepy eyes blinked open. "Do you often watch me slumber?"

"I think best when you are near."

"I'm too tired this morn to spar with you."

Landon wrapped Bronwyn's tresses about his finger.

"Should I have Peyton inform Mary that you will skip lessons today?"

"Absolutely not." His wife bolted upright and swung her legs over the edge of the bed. Her long brown waves swished back and forth against the pale skin of her soft back as she twisted about.

"What are you searching for, wife?"

"My shift."

Admiring the view, he kept silent as Bronwyn stood and turned to rifle through the bedclothes. She placed her hands on her hips. "Do you happen to know where it is, my lord?"

The flush across her chest had his hands itching to reach out for her. He reluctantly paused his admiration of her glorious body. "I might." He grinned.

Bronwyn's eyes focused on the spot on his cheek where his blasted dimple resided. "You might. Was it not you who once said that evasiveness merely results in prolonged cross-examination?" Crawling on to the bed, Bronwyn tugged away the coverlet and sheets that kept him warm.

"I don't recall having said that. However, it does make sense."

Seated on her heels, her knees barely touching his side, Bronwyn lowered her gaze inch by inch until it landed upon his fully aroused member. It wasn't her glorious body that had blood rushing to his groin. It was the wordplay that had him at the ready.

Bronwyn raised her curious eyes to his. "How is it

you never tire? You claim to have a lung condition, yet I am the one left breathless."

"Mayhap your attentions have healed me. Would you care to test my hypothesis?" Landon replaced his hands back behind his head, unwilling to negate the progress he had made the night before. His cock twitched, drawing his wife's attention. She shifted, her brown tresses flowing down her back—tempting him.

Bronwyn ran a hand straight down from his navel to cup his testicles and rolled them in her palm. Looking over her shoulder, she asked, "Do you or do you not know where my shift is?"

He cleared his throat. "I do."

Bending over him, lowered herself until her mouth was mere inches from the tip of his shaft. "If I let you have your way with me, will you tell me where it is?" She circled the head of his cock with her tongue.

With a groan, he replied, "I'll give it to you this minute if that is what you wish. I'll not delay you if you wish to leave."

"And what about you...your discomfort?"

"Wife, I've seen to it many a time. Do you wish to leave?"

Bronwyn took him into her mouth. He pressed his head further into his palms, preventing him from threading his fingers in her hair. Their first night of marriage, he had managed to learn many of Bronwyn's preferences. Stroking and tugging upon her hair was one of her favorites.

At the swirl of her tongue, he let out a low moan. He couldn't take any more without having his hands on her. He reached for her hips and shimmied under her, positioning her pretty, wet slit in front of him. A hand on each hip, he licked at her center. He started with long strokes of his tongue and progressed to circling and flicking her until her hips began to rotate. Her moans of delight set the pace for how fast or slow he moved his tongue over her.

Sliding one hand along her side, he reached between them to cup her breast and play with her nipple. Bronwyn continued to glide her mouth up and down his shaft, altering the pressure of her lips and how deep she would swallow him. His own hips jerked forward as his body sought release, but first, he needed to ensure his wife reached satisfaction. Gripping her bottom, he inched a finger closer to his mouth. His forefinger slid into her channel while his tongue flickered over her core. Bronwyn released him as she gasped. She was close. He kneaded her breast, and he continued to pump his finger as Bronwyn took him back into her mouth. If he pinched her nipple or tugged on her hair, she would reach her peak. He had played extensively with her nipples the night before, so he released his hold on her breast and wrapped his wrist and hand in her long tresses. Pressure mounted in his loins, and he reactively tugged on Bronwyn's hair. Her muscles immediately tightened about his finger, and he ejaculated into her mouth. He untangled his hand from her hair and ran his hand along her spine.

"Hmm." Bronwyn collapsed onto her side. "Perhaps I'll have to adjust the order of my preferences."

Chuckling, Landon retrieved his wife's flimsy shift from under his pillow and placed it against her hip.

Bronwyn grabbed her shift. "Lady Mary is going to have my head. A lady must be neither too early nor late. Punctuality dictates if one will receive an intimate invitation to tea or dinner rather than an invitation along with the masses to a ball or soiree." She pulled the shift overhead and swung her legs over the side of the bed.

"Speaking of engagements." Landon sat up and leaned back against the bed's headboard. "It is time we formally celebrate our union."

Bronwyn's back and shoulders stiffened. "We are to return to London?"

If he could see her expressive face, he'd know how best to answer. She jumped from the bed and spun to glare at him. "But I'm not ready. Lady Mary and I have barely begun."

Bronwyn's heaving chest, nipples pressed tightly against her shift, had his full attention. Her protests registered in the depths of his mind, but his body responded first. Blinking away his wayward thoughts, he hauled the tangled sheets up to his waist and smoothed out the material. "Not London."

Bronwyn narrowed her eyes. Pleased she had freely expressed her opinions, albeit nonverbally, Landon ignored his body's desire to haul her back to bed. "Archbroke has kindly invited us, the Network elders, and a few close friends, to convene at his country estate. We are expected to arrive by week's end."

Head tilted, Bronwyn asked, "Are you sure my dad accepted the invitation?"

"Why wouldn't he?"

"I'd not count on my dad agreeing to leave London to attend such an event." She shook her head and padded over to a fallen pillow.

"But you're his daughter..." The pillow hit him square in the chest.

Hands on her hips, Bronwyn said, "My dad is proud of me; of that I have no doubt. He fully supported the decision for us to marry, but he will not change his ways and hobnob with your lot."

"My lot?" His papa was a second son; the likelihood of him inheriting the Hadfield title had been a distant possibility until Theo's brother died four years past without having married or sired an heir. Who the bloody hell did she consider his lot? It certainly wasn't the lords who lounged about White's all day.

Bronwyn sighed and let her hands fall to her sides. "My dad is a tradesman and a loyal PORF supporter. He has sworn to protect and serve. He'll not elevate himself above what he deems his appointed position." His wife's voice resolute. "Once my dad places the mark upon me, he'll no longer view me as his daughter but as a PORF." Bronwyn touched the harp upon her bracelet and blinked back tears.

Landon reached out for her and she padded closer to the bed.

Holding Bronwyn's hand, he said, "When I asked you to marry me, I didn't know of your ties to the

Network. And since then, I've failed to take into consideration the full ramifications of our union." He raised their joined hands and kissed the back of her hand. "I acted selfishly. I let my love for you blind me."

Her mouth fell wide open. "Did you *say* you love me?"

How could she not know the depth of his feelings for her? Her dubious expression confirmed his failure to show Bronwyn how he felt. His breath caught in his throat, but he managed to eke out, "I did." He wanted Bronwyn to return the sentiment, but she stood blinking as if his confession of love was the most befuddling thing she'd ever heard.

There was a scratch at the door, followed by Peyton's harried voice. "Bronwyn. Blast it. I mean, my lady. Lady Mary is waiting in the morning room."

They couldn't dally any longer. "You'd best go get ready." Landon kissed his dazed wife. "As soon as I'm decent, I'll let your maid in to assist." He turned Bronwyn by the shoulders and gave her rear a pat.

She took three steps forward before she swiveled back around and said, "I...I don't..."

He couldn't bear to hear the truth. Bronwyn didn't love him. Landon interrupted his wife and said, "Mary hates to be kept waiting."

A deep frown replaced Bronwyn's confused features. Turning on her heel, Bronwyn strode to the connecting chamber without another word. Landon leaped from the bed and hastily donned his breeches and shirt.

Damnation.

He was no coward. He'd hear the truth now. Striding to the door, he opened it to reveal an overwrought Peyton wringing her hands.

Taking pity on the poor maid, he said, "Please inform Lady Mary that your mistress will be along shortly." The maid bobbed and then rushed down the hall.

Landon leaned against the closed door and counted to thirty.

Always loved by those close to him, he had misconstrued Bronwyn's enthusiastic responses to him as affection. The barrister in him needed to gain all the facts in order to determine how to move forward. If she didn't care for him, he'd be patient. Perhaps over time, she could learn to love him. He pushed off the door and stood up straight. Taking a deep breath, he fortified himself for the worst. His sluggish feet dragged to the connecting changing chamber.

CHAPTER SIXTEEN

*B*ronwyn stood in the center of the changing chamber, hands clenched at her side, repeating the words *Inhale, Exhale.* He must think her a simpleton, standing next to him gaping like a fool. Every night he mumbled his love for her in his sleep, and she practiced her own admission. Only hours before, she had easily managed a confession of her love. She'd been rattled at having revealed her deep fear of being distanced from everything and everyone she knew, but that was no excuse for her idiotic behavior. Landon had whittled away her defenses. Her fear of appearing weak or ignorant had dissipated.

The colors of her dresses and gowns became a blur in front of her. Tears threatened to spill as she reached for her favorite sky-blue day dress. Thank goodness she was alone. Eyes closed, she inhaled and froze.

"Will you allow me the pleasure of assisting you?"

Landon's deep voice reverberated through her body.

She swiveled to face her husband, who stood on the threshold with his arms loosely crossed. His musky, woodsy smell radiated throughout the small space. His words were spoken casually but there was nothing blithe about the way his stare penetrated her.

She nodded. When he was an arm's length away, she searched for a glimpse of his dimple. It was missing. She swallowed the knot of apprehension that had lodged in her throat and blurted, "Did you know I fancied you back when you were a barrister?"

"I hadn't a clue." Landon uncrossed his arms.

Clutching her hands together in front of her, Bronwyn said, "Remember the day you proposed, and you told me that I had remained in your thoughts?"

Landon took a step closer and settled his warm hands on her hips. "Aye, I recall that day vividly."

Before she lost her nerve, she said, "Well, I confess, there hasn't been a day since the first day I met you that I've not thought about you."

Landon's features softened a tad. "Is that so?"

She couldn't tell if he was baiting her or teasing her. What was his purpose? Bronwyn answered, "Yes. But the man I fantasized about daily was a barrister driven to uphold the law. A man that I could work alongside."

"You envisioned a partnership like your parents share." The quizzical tilt of his brow, and the intensity of his gaze marked his words as a question rather than a statement. It was as if he was trying to read her mind. His lips slowly curved into a grin, and the irresistible dimple she desperately wanted to see appeared. He tucked a wayward lock of hair behind her ear. "You know, I'm the same man as I was before I inherited the title and the mark."

"No. You're not." The man before her set her blood on fire. She placed a hand on his hip inches above the mark. "You are..."

He bent down and kissed her, sending her thoughts scattering. She snaked her arms about his waist and tilted her head as he trailed kisses along her neck. "I can't think straight when you kiss me."

"Don't think." Landon's fingers dug into her bottom as he drew her closer. "What do you feel?"

She chuckled. "All of you at the moment."

His arousal oddly reinforced his earlier statement of love. It wasn't pure lust. The dense energy radiating from him was drenched with the emotion she now recognized as love.

Landon gave her a playful swat on the bottom, causing moisture to pool between her legs. She found she rather liked revealing the rogue within him.

His hand rubbed away the sting.

What could she say to provoke him to repeat the action? "I'm not sure what to call these sensations that you cause within me." She ran her hands up along the sides of his lean body, over his chest and his shoulders, until they came to rest behind his neck. "My body aches to be near you. I think about you constantly."

He groaned as she raised up on her tiptoes, and her stomach grazed against his arousal.

Landon nipped the lobe of her ear. "What else?" Both his hands slid to her bottom.

With a slight hop, she wrapped her legs about his waist. "Take me to back to bed, and I'll tell you all."

Devilishly he raised an eyebrow and asked, "What about your lessons?"

"Why bother? You will merely set out to prove them pointless."

He carried her out of the dressing chamber and paused by the door that led to the hallway. Landon whispered, "Make sure no one is out there to hear you."

She released the latch, and through a sliver of a gap, she peered out into the hall.

Peyton swiveled as the door creaked open. Confused, her maid lifted her eyebrows. "My lady?"

In her husband's arms, Bronwyn was inches higher than her natural height. Smiling, she said, "Please advise Lady Mary that Lord Hadfield has decided to stay abed today. Abiding by yesterday's lesson, it is my duty to sit by his bedside and attend to his every whim." She swallowed a yelp as her husband deliciously smacked her backside.

"Should we send for a physician?"

Her maid's concerned frown evoked enough guilt within Bronwyn to answer solemnly, "No need. I'm certain he merely needs a few hours extra rest."

Payton squinted downward and then gasped. Wide-eyed, she quickly bobbed and fled.

Her maid was an innocent. *Whatever had she seen?*

Landon chuckled, "I'll expect that the entire staff will be aware that their master has hairy legs."

Bronwyn burst out laughing as she shut the door, causing her husband's engorged member to rub against her core. She wiggled and extracted a heated groan from the man she loved. She hadn't managed to say the words out loud, but now that she had his attention for the rest of the day, she would ensure her husband learned how much he meant to her. As Landon carried her to the bed, she placed kisses along his jaw.

"Wife, behave. You and I are to finish our discussion first." He released his hold on her.

As soon as her bottom touched the mattress, she scrambled under the covers. As Landon slid into bed, she snuggled along his side. Her hand came to rest upon his chest.

Peering up at him through her lashes, Bronwyn confessed, "It's hard to define or express the rioting sensations that you cause within both my mind and body."

His Adam's apple bobbed up and down. Landon licked his lips. Whatever he was about to say, she sensed it was hard for him to convey. "Do you regret marrying me?"

Leaning up on her elbow, she shook her head adamantly. "No." One hand on his cheek, she took a deep breath. "Eight years ago, I dreamed of being a barrister's wife. Even then, I considered a union between us as a lofty, crazy wish. When you inherited the earldom, it became an impossibility. Then you became the head PORF, and I knew it was a hopeless fantasy." She leaned over and placed her hand over his heart. "When you proposed, all that came to mind were the reasons I should not marry you."

Landon covered her hand with his. "Then why did you agree?"

"Because I love you." She dropped her mouth to his and infused the kiss with all the emotion she had kept bottled up.

Gasping for air, Landon drew back, "Did you *say* you love me?"

Her husband's roles and responsibilities may have changed, but he was still a barrister at heart. She grinned and said, "I did, counsel, I did."

Solving the puzzle of how to aid him as earl and PORF would have to wait. Today, she was going to indulge in marital relations until her husband was the one to tire first.

CHAPTER SEVENTEEN

*E*xhausted, Landon laid the white strip of material that was once his cravat over his thigh and attempted to smooth out the wrinkles. Shaking his head, he wrapped it around his neck and tied a simple knot that Jacobs would find appalling. Since his wife's declaration of love, the woman was tireless. He hoped his increased stamina was from the surge of invincibility he experienced when Bronwyn was close and not the clean country air. Landon eyed his wife as she readjusted her gown over her delectable breasts. Mindlessly, he grabbed his waistcoat that laid haphazardly on the opposite bench. It was still a two-day journey to London, but he could feel the weight of his responsibilities already encroaching upon him.

Jostled sideways as the coach turned off the dirt path, Landon begrudgingly shifted away from Bronwyn, whose cheeks blazed red as she hastily righted her coiffeur. He pulled back the coach window curtain. Archbroke's manor was impressively well kept.

Squinting, Landon made out a familiar silhouette. "Theo is eagerly awaiting us. She's bouncing on her toes like she used to when my family would visit hers at Hadfield Hall."

Bronwyn huffed. "I'm certain Lady Archbroke would do no such thing. That would be breaking at least three of Mary's rules."

He leaned back and held the curtain open for his wife to see for herself that his highly respected cousin was indeed behaving like a child on Christmas morn. When she remained frozen at the window, Landon said, "I'm not one to tout when I'm correct..." He stopped midsentence as he took in Bronwyn's strained features.

"The mansion is enormous. Significantly larger than Waterford's castle. However am I to navigate such a monstrosity?"

"I expect you'll manage without much of an issue. It's a fairly simple structure, similar to Hadfield Hall—both buildings are easy to commandeer."

"Maybe for you. But it took me three days to memorize Waterford's castle. I won't tell you how many times I opened the door to the water closet, believing it be the door to our chambers."

"Easy mistake. You were only two doors off. I made the same mistake myself when I first visited." Landon chuckled.

The coach door opened. Eager to stretch his legs, Landon jumped out first. Holding out his hand for Bronwyn, he waited for her to exit. When she didn't immediately appear, he stuck his head back into the vehicle.

"Are you going to remain in here all day?"

Bronwyn fiddled with her skirts. "No."

"I promise Archbroke won't bite."

"It's not Lord Archbroke. I've conversed with the man many a time at my dad's store. It's that I dearly want to impress Lady Archbroke and..."

He reached for Bronwyn's hand. "Theo is the sweetest person I know, and she happens to be my favorite cousin."

"I'm certain she is lovely, kind, and the epitome of what all ladies strive to be. But Lady Archbroke is highly regarded and holds an extraordinary place in the hearts of those in the Network—especially the women."

The mix of awe and nervousness in Bronwyn's voice was befuddling. "While I consider Theo an angel for having married Archbroke, she is no demi-god. She is human just like you and I. Shall we go meet our hosts before Theo has my head for making her wait?"

Bronwyn grinned and took his hand. "As you wish."

He gave her a wink. "Perhaps after the introductions I shall show you the way to our chambers."

Barely audible foot falls had Landon rolling his shoulders back and preparing himself to great his cousin.

"Landon!" Theo's voice was mere inches away.

He instinctively hauled his wife to his side.

Theo looked down her nose at him, despite the fact he was at least twelve inches taller than her. "Why are the two of you dawdling?"

He swiveled around to find Theo flanked by Waterford and Mary, both with smirks on their faces. During the last leg of their trip, he had limited his attention to kissing...though not all the kissing had occurred upon Bronwyn's delightfully shaped lips that had curled into a smile.

Bronwyn stepped forward and curtsied. What was she doing? Theo should be the one paying respect to Bronwyn since she outranked Theo. Placing a hand under her elbow, he guided her to stand next to him, except he was barreled out of the way as Theo threw her arms about Bronwyn.

"Cousin!" Theo pulled back and grabbed his wife's hands. "Welcome to the family. Aunt Henrietta and Christopher are not due to arrive until tomorrow. I selfishly wanted to spend the day with you." Theo's bright emerald green eyes landed on Landon. "She's all mine for the day. You kept me waiting, and now you will pay."

With a nod, Landon conceded. He was no fool—Theo was treated by both the Network and PORFs as queen, regardless of the rondure.

Theo led Bronwyn away. Separated from his wife by a few feet, and he already missed her.

A pebble hit him square in the middle of his back. Landon swiveled and caught the second one before it hit him in the chest. He stared at his cousin-in-law, Graham Drummond, Earl of Archbroke and Head of the Home Office, as he sauntered up the drive. Landon blinked twice. The man who the ton had once considered a dandy, as immaculate in appearance as his manor, now resembled a field hand with his hair disheveled and clad in sweaty breeches and lawn shirt.

Archbroke said, "About bloody time you came to relieve me of your duties. I've had little to no spare time to spend with Theo."

"For which I believe Theo is thankful."

"Hardly. The woman is in her second trimester and has regained her..." Archbroke blinked and then shut his mouth tight.

Since Landon's proposal to Bronwyn, the woman had occupied his thoughts every moment. Love was incredibly distracting. If Archbroke was as preoccupied as Landon was with how to get his wife back into bed, Landon certainly did not want to hear whatever it was Archbroke was about to impart.

Archbroke came to stand next to him. Footmen scurried about unloading the numerous trunks both Mary and Bronwyn deemed necessary. Long gone were the days of traveling with a single travel bag and one other. Bronwyn was well worth the tradeoff.

Landon asked, "Where were you when we arrived?"

Archbroke wiped a bead of sweat from his temple. "Out running."

"Running where?"

"Nowhere in particular; about the estate." Archbroke turned to mount the steps leading up to the front doors. "Theo's been hounding me to inform you that Cadby declined my invitation to attend the house party and has summoned Bronwyn to come home."

His father-in-law's rejection of a request by a PORF

stunned him despite Bronwyn's forewarning. But it was the notoriously difficult man's demand that his daughter return home that rocked Landon to his heels. "Whatever for?"

"As your wife, she must receive the mark. Cadby insists it be done sooner rather than later, and he will not recognize your union until it is done."

Archbroke entered the manor, glanced at a door down the hall, and then to the staircase. It was the first time Landon had ever witnessed the man hesitate.

"Are there any other matters that I should be aware of?" Landon asked.

"No."

"What's the problem, then?"

"I want to greet your new wife and see mine, but I know I need to bathe first. I'm trying to decide which action would please Theo more. She's probably already miffed I didn't return before you arrived."

Landon grinned. Married over a year, and Theo still was Archbroke's number one priority. Now that he was married, he sympathized with the man, for Landon couldn't imagine a day in which Bronwyn's happiness wouldn't come before his own.

Waterford exited the room Archbroke had just been eying. As he approached, it became apparent the man had fled. His hair was in disarray, and he tugged at his neatly tied cravat. Walking right past them, Waterford said, "I need a drink."

Archbroke bounded up the stairs, and Landon followed Waterford to the library.

"What the devil is the matter?" Landon asked as Waterford poured a healthy finger of brandy into a glass.

"More etiquette lessons, except now Lady Theo is in charge."

Landon groaned. He'd have his work cut out for him tonight, for Bronwyn would likely take Theo's word as gospel.

CHAPTER EIGHTEEN

*M*arching back and forth in Theo's lavish bedchamber, temporarily reassigned to her, Bronwyn counted backward from one hundred to calm her nerves. Her ability to recall facts and dates rarely failed her but remembering to whom she had and had not been formally introduced to was daunting. As a member of the Network, she was expected to memorize the names and faces of those that interacted with PORFs for years. She prayed she wouldn't get confused and inadvertently cut a member of the ton.

Fustian!

Stopping in front of a full-length looking glass, Bronwyn practiced what she hoped was a graceful ballroom curtsy since that was where she anticipated most of her introductions to occur. The slightest difference in how far she bent at the knee dictated if she performed the curtsy correctly or not. She'd never considered herself graceful. Her strides were purposeful and firm despite having practiced ad nauseum.

Under the tutelage of Mary, Theo, and her warm, loving mother-in-law, who had arrived two days prior, Bronwyn had managed to master the act of nodding. She'd never given thought to the speed or angle of her nods, but according to her mentors, that gesture could communicate displeasure, urgency, or pleasure all dependent upon the situation and execution. Despite her progress, Bronwyn was no more confident she would be accepted by Landon's peers and their wives than when she began. No matter how many times Mary, Theo, or her mother-in-law reassured her she was ready, the niggling fear of being found lacking plagued Bronwyn.

In addition, Landon's nightly reassurances she should behave as she pleased, and that everyone would simply fall in love with her as he had, didn't ring true. Granted, it hadn't taken her long to gain her cousin-by-marriage's full support or Mary's, but Mary was sworn by duty to assist her, and Theo never discriminated against anyone. She unconditionally gave her love and guidance to all.

The noise of houseguests out on the lawn wafted through the window. Guests had begun to arrive two days ago, but in a desperate play for time, Bronwyn had convinced Theo that it would be best she remained unseen, unannounced until the last guest arrived. She was still uncertain exactly how she had managed such a feat. When Landon learned of the plan, a heated debate ensued between the two cousins. They volleyed opinions at each other quicker than a blink. In the end, Theo ended all discussion by stating, "It's your wife's wish."

When Landon looked to Bronwyn for confirmation, she had nodded. A flash of disappointment crossed his features, and then he announced, "Very well. We will introduce my wife to everyone on the evening the last guest arrives. We shall have a celebratory dinner."

For the last two nights, Landon had joined her for supper. The first night, Landon discussed his investments with the other lords and sought her opinion on several matters that impacted the running of the Hadfield estate. On the second, he revealed his concerns over the shift in power within the Royal Court which could have significant impact on the Network. He didn't badger her into agreeing with him. Instead, Landon always gave thanks for her views and informed her they were important to him. It gave her hope that she might become as valuable to him as her mum was to her dad. Regardless of the topics discussed over their meal, Landon ensured neither of them fell asleep until they were both delightfully sated and physically exhausted.

Peyton rushed into their chambers and pulled back the curtains, exposing bright rays of sunlight. "My lady. The Earl and Countess of Devonton will be arriving today. That means no more hiding!"

Bronwyn swirled away from the mirror and strode over to the window to catch a glimpse of the renowned Lady Lucy. But there was no sign of the Devonton coach.

Visualizing the guest list she had memorized, her palms began to sweat. The Network monitored the activities of many, and while Bronwyn was privy to the extensive reports, she'd never had reason to meet any of the individuals mentioned in them—until now.

Mary had provided entertaining commentary on each person and at least one distinct trait for each to assist Bronwyn in identifying them. However, she found it easier to recall details when she compartmentalized information. Bronwyn mentally grouped the guests into three categories: those associated with the Home Office, Foreign Office, and the Network. However, two couples didn't fall neatly into a single category.

Matthew Stanford, Marquis of Harrington, formally a dual agent of the Home and Foreign Offices, and his wife, Lady Grace, who was the acting head of the Foreign Office. Both had recently pledged allegiance and were now members of the Network. Bronwyn decided it best to place the couple along with Waterford and Mary in the Network set.

Blake Gower, Earl of Devonton, agent of the Foreign Office. His wife, Lucille Stanford Gower, Countess Devonton, worked for the Home Office. Neither husband nor wife were directly associated with the Network, which left Bronwyn undecided how to best assign the couple—they were in a category of their own.

Mary had described Lady Lucy as a short, blonde beauty with a sweet smile and a razor-sharp mind, while her husband Lord Devonton was tall and deceptively handsome, with the uncanny ability to recall the minutest of details. Lord and Lady Devonton were the last couple to arrive and intrigued her the most. And their arrival meant she must reveal her presence.

Bronwyn released the window coverings, padded over to the enormous bed, and let herself flop backward onto the soft mattress. Inhaling deeply, she sat up and found herself face to face with a striking pink silk gown.

"Emma's creations are divine." Peyton's smile was infectious, and Bronwyn found her own lips curling at the corners.

She admired the modest lace trimmed square décolleté with matching lace on the edges of the puffed sleeves. Her best friend had not failed to deliver on her promise. The elegant yet uncomplicated dress suited Bronwyn perfectly. And the shimmering pink silk—a material any woman would be mad not to covet. She bounded up from the bed, her confidence bolstered by the prospect of wearing the gown. Peyton lifted the garment, lining up the cap sleeves with Bronwyn's shoulders.

If I look like a lady and act like a lady, surely no one will care I am a shopkeeper's daughter at heart.

Her heart faltered. She'd never been ashamed of her lineage before. Why was she attempting to be someone she was not? No dress would mask her true nature, Bronwyn sidestepped around Peyton and headed for the washbowl in the corner of the room. "I think I might like a bath before donning the gown. Can you arrange it?"

"Yes, my lady." Peyton bobbed and headed for the door. "I shall take the dress and have it pressed...again."

The door clicked closed. Bronwyn rested her hands

on either side of the porcelain basin and inhaled a steadying breath. The dark smudges under her eyes rippled in her reflection. She needed a few more hours of rest before being paraded in front of the guests. Crawling into the bed, she pulled the pillow over her head and blocked out the sounds of the house party.

HIDDEN BENEATH THE BED LINENS, Bronwyn kept her eyes closed as the sound of water being poured into what she hoped was to be her bath filled the room. Her head still felt heavy, but she was no longer sleepy.

"The footmen have left, my lady; you can come out now." Peyton's words reminded Bronwyn of the days when the two of them used to play hide and go seek as children. It was time she grew up and faced facts—she was a lady now. Best to start acting like one.

Pushing back the covers, Bronwyn rolled out of bed. "How long have I been asleep?"

"It's nearly time for tea. You've slept all day, my lady." Peyton lathered up soap in a washcloth and held it at the ready. She looked at the soapy material and then back to Bronwyn. "Oh, do you need help getting..."

Bronwyn awkwardly bent her arm behind her back and tried to reach for the row of buttons of her day dress. "I'm not a babe. I'm fully capable of undressing and bathing myself."

Peyton's chin fell to her chest. Blast. She hadn't meant to take out her frustration on her friend. That was not well done. Hadn't Theo said a lady was always kind to all, no matter their station or role within a household?

Bronwyn crept up to her maid. "I'm sorry, Willa. I should not have lashed out at you. I would really appreciate your help."

Spinning Bronwyn about by the shoulders, Peyton said, "It's a good thing I've known ye long enough to know that ye hate relying on others. But ye are a lady now and these..." Peyton deftly released the row of buttons and then tugged at the laces on Bronwyn's corset. "Ye need me to get ye in and out of these contraptions."

"Aye, Peyton, I need *you*." Stepping out of her dress and into the tub, Bronwyn said, "I've always been self-sufficient. Having everyone on hand...waiting on me... watching to see what error I'll make next..." A jug of water fell over her head and face. Spluttering, Bronwyn turned to glare at her maid.

"Ye are a fool if ye really believe anyone in the Network would be thinking like that. Open yer eyes. Ye're surrounded by us, those ye have led within the Network. If we are over attentive, it is because we want to see ye happy and succeed. We believe in ye, Bronwyn Cadby Neale, and we couldn't be prouder to serve ye as Countess of Hadfield."

Bronwyn's eyes welled with tears.

Peyton handed her a washcloth. "Ye know, it's an adjustment for me too. It's the first time I've ever had to sleep in a bed all to meself." Peyton's family had lived next door to Bronwyn's. Four years Bronwyn's junior, Peyton was one of five children.

"That must be scary, sleeping all alone."

"Oh, no. It's not scary. It's wonderful." Peyton smiled. "I like not waking up to a foot or an elbow in my ribs."

They both let out a giggle.

Peyton sobered and said, "Ye know..." Her maid ran the soapy cloth over Bronwyn's shoulders. "If I didn't believe in ye, I'd never have applied to be yer maid. Ye are an inspiration to many of us girls. Ye was the first to convince the Network elders that unmarried female members could be contributors and not merely procreators. And ye did so before Lady Theo inherited and proved to all ye were right."

It was true. Bronwyn had waged war with her dad in order to gain permission to work at Landon's legal firm. If she could win over the Network elders, certainly she could do the same with the dozen or so guests under Archbroke's roof.

The clack of heels came to a halt outside Bronwyn's door. As Peyton scurried to see who it was, a note appeared at the base of the door and slid through the small opening.

Her maid picked it up and read it. "Lord Hadfield is awaiting you in Lord Archbroke's study."

"Guess I best not make him wait." Bronwyn placed a hand on the sides of the tub and began to stand.

Peyton shook her head. "Oh, no. I'm going to wash, dry, and brush that hair until it shines. And you are going to scrub your skin clean like we were taught."

An hour later, Bronwyn stared at the woman in the looking glass. Peyton peeked over her shoulder and winked. The pink silk dress fell perfectly to the ground in simple, elegant lines. Her hands began to sweat in her white elbow-length gloves.

With a deep sigh, Bronwyn said, "Wish me luck."

"It's not luck ye will be needing." Peyton gave her a push toward the door. "A steel will to resist that husband of yours and ensure he doesn't muss up your coiffure before dinner."

Over her shoulder, Bronwyn answered, "I'll be sure to tell his lordship it was you who ordered him to keep his hands to himself." With a wink, she shut the door.

Practically skipping down the hall, she rounded the corner and quickly checked to make sure no one was about. She shifted a painting of Lord Archbroke's great-great grandfather and stuck her finger in what appeared to be a knot in the wood paneling, but was in reality access to the latch of the secret passageway. Carefully repositioning the painting, Bronwyn slid into the narrow passageway and closed the entrance door. Thank goodness she wasn't afraid of confined spaces or the dark. Theo had shown her how to access all the secret passages built into the mansion, informing her that the ones at Hadfield Hall were all similarly located and connected the same rooms. As a child, Theo had loved discovering the false walls and intricate latches, only to be disappointed when she married Lord Archbroke and learned all three PORF family country estates were built in the same fashion. It was all new to Bronwyn, and she reveled in the clandestine nature of the designs.

She pushed on the door that led to the study. As she

stepped through the exit, an arm wrapped about her waist, and her back came into contact with the warm, hard chest of her husband.

Landon's lips landed softly on the crook of her neck slightly below her ear. "I was about to give up waiting and come get you."

"You—give in? Never."

Landon chucked and placed another kiss upon her sensitive skin. Bronwyn tilted her neck to allow him better access, but then Peyton's parting words floated through her mind, and she stiffened and pulled out of his embrace. "Impatient to parade me before the piranhas?"

"I wouldn't allow any such creatures near you." Landon's eyebrows knit together as he moved past her toward the door. "I don't claim they don't exist, and we will come in contact with them when we return to London, but here, tonight, you will meet those I consider friends."

Landon's cool tone left no doubt she had disappointed and offended her husband. Bronwyn was about to apologize when the door swung open. An attractive lady with dark mahogany hair barreled into Landon. Since it wasn't Theo nor Mary, Bronwyn ducked behind her husband to avoid detection.

Landon's hands shot out to steady the stranger, who he greeted. "Lady Grace."

Ah. The elusive Foreign Secretary.

Slightly out of breath, Lady Grace said, "Lord Hadfield, I apologize."

Unexpectedly Landon shifted to his right, and

Bronwyn quickly drew her skirts closer about her, but she wasn't sure if she had succeeded in hiding her presence.

Lady Grace said, "I was looking for Matthew."

Landon moved again, this time back to his left, his heel landing on her toes.

"Ow!" Bronwyn slapped her hand over her mouth. Blast! Hiding behind her husband was not the first impression Bronwyn wanted to make on Lady Grace.

A giggle escaped Lady Grace before she asked, "Aren't you going to make the proper introductions?"

Bronwyn and Landon simultaneously answered, "No." Their adamant reply hung in the air.

Apparently, her husband was content to remain silent. Bronwyn cleared her throat and said, "I apologize, Lady Grace. Landon and I didn't mean to raise our voices."

Landon added, "Harrington is currently elsewhere."

"If you should see my husband, would you be so kind as to inform him I would like to have a word with him?"

Interesting. Lady Grace had employed the same approach with Landon that Theo often utilized in order to obtain the cooperation of another. She had phrased a command in the form of a question. Bronwyn made a mental note to remember the strategy, for it must be reasonably effective if both ladies employed it.

Landon answered, "I'm not one of your agents you can order about."

Her husband's curt reply was not what Lady Grace deserved. Bronwyn poked him hard in the middle of his back, causing Landon to roll forward onto his toes and take a half step forward. "Landon, don't be daft!"

Theo's voice came flooding to the forefront of her mind. *Men are partial to honey and highly averse to vinegar.*

She tried again. "Landon, will you please ensure Lord Harrington finds *his wife* in the hothouse."

Landon nodded.

"My thanks to you...both." Lady Grace's skirts rustled, and this time Bronwyn was ready for Landon's movements and mirrored them so as not to reveal herself.

The door closed, and Landon whirled about with a broad grin on his face.

CHAPTER NINETEEN

*F*inally, Bronwyn's true nature had reappeared. Confirmation his efforts each night were not futile and offered more than pure carnal pleasure.

The dimple that typically wielded no power over his wife's constitution appeared with his grin, and the frown that had marred her pretty features was replaced with a smile.

"You were magnificent!" Landon wrapped Bronwyn up in a hug and kissed the top of her head.

He wanted to twirl her about and celebrate. He couldn't wait to introduce her to everyone at dinner. "Theo and Mary may still be at tea. Did you want to join them and become acquainted with the other ladies before I announce our union at dinner?"

The gentle curve of Bronwyn's lips thinned into a line. "I'd prefer to take this opportunity to discuss a few issues which have plagued me since our arrival here."

With her days centered upon the ridiculous etiquette lessons, Landon hadn't even considered she may have other concerns. "What matters have you worried?"

Bronwyn moved to occupy Archbroke's worn leather chair behind the desk. She motioned for him to sit across from her on the other side of the table. Bronwyn's relaxed, calm demeanor portended trouble. The muscles in the back of his neck and shoulders tensed.

The minx leaned forward, distracting him. Lacing her fingers, she rested her hands in front of her on the desk and met Landon's gaze. "All of the Network elders, except Waterford, declined Lord Archbroke's invitation to attend the gathering."

"They are following your dad's example and standing in solidarity behind his decision not to attend."

"Does it not concern you that a PORF's request was not immediately seen to?"

"The act of defiance in this instance is under-standable."

"How so? Those very elders taught me, it is of the utmost importance to obey and assist all PORFs no matter our own personal beliefs, for we were not always privy to all the facts."

"Your dad's demand that you receive the mark as soon as possible is out of genuine concern for you. I cannot blame the man for his actions, for if you were my daughter, I too would have declined Archbroke's invitation."

"Reasonable or not, his act of defiance is not accept-able. I will not let him, nor the other elders, undermine your leadership nor the requests of the other PORFs. I'd like to send correspondence to my dad reminding him of his oath and pledge to honor *all* PORF requests and inform him we expect him and the other elders to be present by week's end."

Landon steepled his fingers under his chin. He wanted to consider the matter before agreeing but also wanted to foster Bronwyn's surge in confidence. "I'll make sure your letter is delivered."

His wife's features lit up. Landon regretted having to add, "However, you should be aware that the House of Lords is set to reconvene by week's end, and if it pleases you, we too will be departing in three days."

"Oh, is there an important matter to be voted upon?"

"Nay. A trial of a peer is to be held. With the influx of new life peers granted by the Crown, many believe it important that those of us who hold hereditary titles participate and be present more often in the House of Lords."

"Very well. I shall simply modify my note to inform my dad to be prepared to dine with us upon our return."

His wife was terrific—fluid, able to make quick rational decisions.

Landon stood.

Bronwyn fluttered her eyelids and said, "Husband, I'm not yet finished."

He let out a chuckle and resumed his seat. "Proceed."

"When we return to London, what am I to do all day?"

He hadn't the slightest idea as to how ladies occupied

their time during the day. "What do Theo and Mary do to occupy their time?"

"Well, let me think." Bronwyn pursed her lips and frowned.

He wanted to haul Bronwyn across the desk and settle her in his lap. Landon stood with the intention to wrap his hands about his wife's waist. Her stony expression halted his movements. She was going to be a formidable leader in her own right. He chose well.

The crease between her eyebrows deepened as she said, "Hmm...Mary made mention of calling upon friends, attending and holding teas, visiting Emma, and sometimes performing investigations for Theo."

"There you have it. You can do the same."

"Really?" Bronwyn stood and walked to the window. "Emma is my only friend, and she is awfully busy with her shop now that her clientele has expanded to many of the ladies of the ton. Who will invite me to tea? Until I've been introduced properly, I can't hold a tea of my own. I highly doubt Theo will trust me to assist with her investigations."

Landon took the opportunity to get close. He sidled up to her. "I will make the proper introductions this evening at dinner. Our salver will be overflowing with invitations before you know it. It's a good thing you have a keen mind for names and faces. As for Theo, I'm certain she trusts you, but since you outrank her, it should be Theo who would run errands for you."

She released a deep sigh. "You hear my plight and offer answers, but you are not listening to me."

What did she mean he wasn't listening?

The dinner bell chimed in the hallway.

Bronwyn's spine stiffened.

He turned her by the shoulders to face him. "I don't understand, but I want to. Will you explain later tonight?"

She searched his eyes, for what he wasn't sure, but then she smiled and her shoulders relaxed.

With a twinkle in her eye, Bronwyn answered, "Aye. I'll attempt to provide clarity as you do each eve."

CHAPTER TWENTY

*R*aising onto her tiptoes, Bronwyn slid her hands up Landon's chest and over his shoulders. Safe and secure in his arms, she was almost convinced the evening would be as easy as dining with the Network elders.

Landon brushed his warm lips along her neck to settle upon her mouth. The sound of footsteps from the hall were no longer the reason for her increased heart rate. The chime of the dinner bell ringing a second time permeated her foggy mind, and her husband released her lips. His hazel eyes bored into her. "Ready?"

Bronwyn stared at his upturned palm. She racked her brain for an excuse to remain where they were. But there were no reasonable reasons to postpone the inevitable any longer. Sliding her hand into his, her heart swelled with a surge of confidence. She nodded, and his warm fingers closed about hers. Landon's lips curved into a smile, complete with the dimple that made her feel giddy.

Together they stood at the threshold of Lord Archbroke's study. Immediately the procession of guests halted, and Landon led Bronwyn to the head of the line. Trained to remain in the shadows and unseen, her pulse raced as she walked by the prying eyes of guests.

Mary's voice echoed through her mind: *Ignore the whispers and avoid making eye contact.* The murmurs of *Who is that?* Were hard to dispel and reinforced the fact she was an outsider.

They entered the grand dining room and Landon squeezed her hand.

Sapphire blue skirts filled Bronwyn's view. "Chin up."

Recognizing Theo's voice, Bronwyn dutifully raised her face. Her husband glared down at his cousin, clearly displeased.

Theo ignored Landon and said, "Cousin, you look magnificent tonight." Theo waved a hand, and a footman appeared. "Larry will show you to your seat while I have a quick word with my dear, beloved cousin."

Nervous about leaving Landon's side, she tightened her grip on her husband's arm.

Landon whispered, "I'll be seated opposite you, to the right of Archbroke. I'll just be a moment."

Theo shook her head. "I'm afraid not. With Prinny's arrival I've had to move the seating arrangements. Bronwyn will be seated to *my* right and you on Archbroke's left."

Dear heaven. What was the Prince Regent doing

here? Theo had lost her mind seating her in the third highest-ranking guest position at the table.

The footman stepped forward and led Bronwyn to her seat. She managed to catch but a few of Theo's agitated words—*Prinny doesn't approve.*

What did the Prince Regent not support? Most likely, the heir to the throne thought her unworthy of Landon. And Bronwyn agreed. Wringing her hands in her lap under the table as the footman pushed in Bronwyn's chair, she glanced to her left. Lady Lucy was as beautiful as the rampant Network rumors had whispered. Petite with shimmering blonde hair and a sweet but mischievous smile. Without an introduction, Bronwyn remained mute and forced the corners of her mouth up in an attempt to mirror Lady Lucy's welcoming expression. Down the table, Bronwyn spied Lord Waterford. His attention was trained on the seat opposite him further down the large dining table, which meant Bronwyn would not be able to see Lady Mary for the duration of the meal.

Lady Lucy chuckled. "Waterford has always been watchful of Mary, but since they married, he detests being more than a foot away from her."

Bronwyn turned to face the woman. "I apologize..."

Lady Lucy casually rested a hand on Bronwyn's forearm. "Countess Hadfield. Theo holds you in very high esteem. I hope you will grant me the honor of addressing you..."

She interrupted the woman and blushed. "Please call me Bronwyn."

The woman's blue-gray eyes twinkled with curiosity. "Lady Bronwyn, allow me to introduce myself. I'm Lucy, and this"—she leaned back and waved a hand at the man seated next to her—"is my husband, Blake. Also known as Earl of Devonton."

"It's an honor to meet you, Lord Devonton, Lady Devonton." The informality of Lady Lucy's introduction caught Bronwyn off guard. The lady had broken at least a half dozen or so etiquette rules.

"Lady Bronwyn, I'd be honored if you called me Blake. We are in the company of good friends...except for our last-minute guest." His brow furrowed into a frown.

Lady Lucy elbowed her husband hard in the ribs. "It's none of our business why the Prince Regent decided to invite himself. Plus, Theo thankfully placed him far from us. We won't be subjected to his nonsense this eve."

"Theo knows you can't hold your tongue, and none of us care to see you imprisoned for offending our dear Prince Regent." The familiar voice had Bronwyn clenching her hands. Lord Hereford was seated across from her. The man was responsible for Emma's rare but devastating bouts of anguish. He had also recently been appointment to the role of Crown advisor, a position previously held by a PORF for generations.

Taking a deep breath, she shifted her regard to the other guests. Where were Christopher and her mother-in-law? Bronwyn had hoped Theo would have seated them nearby.

Theo glided up to the table and took her seat. As if reading her mind, Theo leaned over and said, "Christopher is seated near Landon, and Aunt Henri has chosen to dine in her rooms tonight."

"Is she unwell?"

"No, as soon as Aunt Henri learned of the Prince Regent's arrival along with his entourage, she declined to join us. She did ask me to pass along her apologies and promises to make it up to you another time."

Unable to hold back her curiosity, Bronwyn asked, "Why is he here?"

Theo's light demeanor disappeared. "I'll leave it to Landon to inform you." Instead of smiling at her guests, who were all unabashedly eavesdropping on their conversation, Theo's lips thinned into a straight line. She glared at the lot of them until they turned their attention to the elegant dining sets placed before them.

Bronwyn scanned the guests seated near them. None of them were privy to the existence of PORFs or the Network. A tendril of unease ran down her spine.

A procession of footmen entered the room and placed bowls of soup in front of each guest. Bronwyn waited for the others to begin eating before she dared to lift her own spoon. Bringing the heavy silver utensil to her mouth, she stilled her shaking hand in order not to spill the onion stock down her chin. The broth was warm and soothing. Bronwyn concentrated on consuming her soup while Lady Lucy regaled her with the events that resulted in their delayed arrival.

Lady Lucy finished with, "We should have arrived sooner, but it took an extraordinary amount of effort for the *men* to fix the broken axle."

Theo smiled and said, "We are simply glad you both arrived safe and sound."

Everyone around her was engrossed in Lady Lucy's tale. Bronwyn scooped another spoonful of soup. With the broth halfway to her mouth, Bronwyn's noticed the near-full bowls of the other guests. In her house, it was rude to leave food uneaten. Placing her spoon to her lips, she managed to swallow the soup that now tasted cold and bitter. The skin on the back of her neck prickled. At the far end of the table, the Prince Regent was glaring at her. She hastily placed her spoon upon the table, and as soon as it hit the linen, footmen stepped up and removed the bowls. Fustian! She had delayed the dinner service.

Chin to her chest, she didn't dare look about. Prinny's angry scowl would forever be burned into her memory. Uniform footsteps and the smell of fish wafted into the room. She loved fish, yet her stomach rolled as the scent permeated the room. Bronwyn blinked back the tears of failure as a square piece of poached salmon, centered on a petite dish and covered with a mousseline sauce, was placed in front of her. Thin slices of cucumber lined the edge of the plate. It was the most intricate appetizer she'd ever seen. Her family was one of a few that could afford three hearty meals a day. But none this elaborate.

Bronwyn scolded herself for having believed Landon's claims that this evening's dinner would be similar to those they had shared with Mary and Gilbert at Waterford's castle. Mary's cook had prepared meals similar to those prepared by her mum, except they were served on fancy plates. Her stomach was in knots. Fear manifested in the form of anger, and Bronwyn scowled at her plate.

Theo's hand rested upon her forearm. "Landon said you loved salmon. Was I misinformed?"

"Oh, no. It's...well, it simply looks too good to be eaten."

A giggle escaped Lucy, and Bronwyn was acutely aware of the chuckles from the men. She hadn't meant to sound like a peagoose.

Bronwyn noticed Lucy staring at Waterford and giggling. The men, too, were preoccupied with the peculiar expression that had settled on Mary's husband's features.

Theo said, "Waterford prefers beef to fish. But don't worry, the man won't go hungry. Two more courses and then he'll be served what his heart desires."

Lady Lucy snorted. "Certainly you don't intend to serve Mary to him in front of our esteemed guest." The quick-witted comment drew chuckles from all the guests within earshot. They all shared a sense of familiarity and comradery.

Bronwyn didn't belong.

She peeked at Lady Lucy from the corner of her eyes. None of the guests seated near them appeared offended or repulsed by Lady Lucy's blatant disregard for propriety. The woman didn't abide by any of the rules Bronwyn had agonized over. A lump formed in Bronwyn's throat. She couldn't imagine herself comfortable, laughing, and making jokes like Lady Lucy with the guests seated at the table.

Bronwyn laid her fork back down upon the table. "I think I'll go check on my mother-in-law."

"There really is no need." Theo placed a bite in her mouth.

"I want to." Bronwyn plastered a look of genuine concern on her face.

Theo dabbed the corners of her mouth with her napkin. "Very well. I'll make an excuse for you if you're not back by the next course. But Landon will want to make the announcement soon, so don't dawdle too long."

A footman assisted her out of her seat and escorted her out to the hall. As soon as they were out of sight, Bronwyn said, "Have a coach readied and waiting for me out back. And Larry, not a word to anyone. Am I clear?"

The footman nodded and dashed off to do her bidding.

She hurried down the hall, up the staircase around two more corridors, and came up short as she passed her mother-in-law's chambers. Frozen, Bronwyn faced the door before her. She wasn't a liar or a coward, but the fear of disappointing her sweet mother-in-law was paralyzing. Before she could flee, the door swung open and the dowager Hadfield stood at the threshold with her hands upon her hips. "What are you about, my dear?"

Under her mother-in-law's piercing gaze, Bronwyn swayed as she shifted her weight from foot to foot. "I don't fit in with his lot."

One eyebrow arched, Landon's mama said, "My son won't give you up that easily."

She would not change her mind. She was leaving.

Hands clenched, Bronwyn said, "I made a mistake. I shouldn't have agreed to marry him."

The older woman wrapped her up in a hug. "I've come to love you as my own daughter. You are no ninny. If this is what you have decided is best, then I shall not be the one to persuade you otherwise. However, before you leave, you must inform me of your destination so I can go to sleep at ease."

Blast. She hadn't considered a destination; only her escape. Bronwyn was released from the woman's warm embrace.

"I shall be going home. Back to London."

"To the Hadfield townhouse or back to your parents?"

Bronwyn smiled as her plans solidified in her mind. "Neither. Don't worry, I'll be safe."

Her mother-in-law frowned. "Tell me where and I'll promise not to say a word."

"Very well, you can find me at Ms. Lennox's shop."

"Will you be leaving a note for Landon?"

"I've not enough time. You'll give me your word not to share with him my whereabouts?"

"You have my promise. However, I'll be more than happy to pass along whatever details you *would* like for me to share."

"Please convey my apologies to Theo, and my thanks to Mary for all her assistance." Bronwyn sighed. "And please tell him...tell Landon that I love him, but it was a mistake for us to marry. I'll make arrangements for an annulment so he can marry a lady more befitting his needs."

Her mother-in-law donned a motherly look and said, "You are wrong. There is no one more deserving or better suited than you, but until you believe it yourself, there is no reason for you to stay." Engulfed in a hug, Bronwyn hugged her mother-in-law back.

She withdrew and said, "Thank you for your help."

Dowager Hadfield shook her head and stepped back into her room. Sad eyes peered back at Bronwyn until the door click closed.

With no time to waste, Bronwyn ran to her rooms and ordered Peyton to pack a valise. It was a solid two-day journey back to London. A Network inn was close by. She'd stay the night there and travel home with the first rays of daylight on the morrow.

She hastily swiped a tear from her cheek. Landon needed a woman who was bold and brilliant like Lady Lucy. Not a wife who behaved like a peagoose in front of his closest friends despite days of etiquette lessons. Bronwyn led her maid through the secret passageways to the back door.

As ordered, the coach was readied and waiting.

The driver asked, "Where to my lady?"

With one foot on the coach steps, Bronwyn answered, "The Lone Dove."

CHAPTER TWENTY-ONE

*F*or the tenth time since his wife left the room, Landon considered Bronwyn's empty seat. Two courses later, he poked the langoustine drizzled in lemon garlic butter with his fork. It was a delicacy he'd hoped Bronwyn would find appetizing.

Seated next to him, Lady Grace raised a napkin to her mouth. "I heard rumors of you leaving town to marry, but I didn't believe them until our earlier encounter. What is Countess Hadfield's name?"

"Lady Bronwyn." His heart sank as he considered her still vacant seat. "I had intended to make the official announcement this eve."

The slight widening of Lady Grace's eyes confirmed he had managed to shock the woman. A grand feat in itself, but he was of no mind to savor the moment. He needed to escape Prinny's company and hunt down his wife.

"Congratulations." Lady Grace returned her napkin

to her lap and turned her attention back to her plate. "Where is she now?"

He had no clue. Initially, Landon had assumed Bronwyn had left to use the necessary and would return, but Theo's nervous glances at the door had him suspicious of her prolonged absence.

"Do you need my assistance?" Lady Grace asked.

Landon wasn't confident what action, if any, he should take. "Not at this time." His nightly efforts to convince Bronwyn she should ignore society dictates and act as she pleased had highlighted for him some of his own hypocrisies. Last night, Bronwyn declared she'd no longer wanted to continue her lessons with his mama, Theo, and Mary. At first, he was overjoyed at the news, but when he questioned her, he discovered Bronwyn's reasoning was due to her distaste for seeking out the help of others and not because she was confident in her abilities. Landon's chest ached with failure. He too despised asking for assistance, but if he was to act, he'd need the help of his cousin, Archbroke.

He turned to face the man who was more like a brother than merely a cousin-by-marriage. Archbroke's features were strained. Prinny's decision to cut his hunting trip short and join the house party to voice his disapproval of the mounting tension between the hereditary and life peers was not well received by anyone, least of all Archbroke.

Archbroke wagged an eyebrow and said, "Go. I'll entertain our esteemed guest."

With stealth learned from his dear cousin, Landon quietly rose and slipped away from the table.

Prinny continued to regale the company with tales of his hunting prowess. "And wouldn't you know, the red-furred beast scurried right in front of me." England was doomed. The man hadn't managed to ensnare a fox twenty feet away from him.

Landon spotted the footman Theo had assigned to his wife walking toward him. When the man noticed him approaching, he swiveled away. Unlike the Prince Regent, Landon was not about to let his prey evade him.

"Stop," Landon commanded. The footman froze.

At the sound of rustling silk behind him, Landon stiffened. Holding his breath, he peered over his shoulder, hoping to see his wife. But it wasn't Bronwyn; it was his mama.

Landon said, "Stay where you are."

His mama stopped in her tracks.

"Not you, mama. I was speaking to the footman."

"But you were looking at me."

Landon sighed. After having slept little the night prior, he had exhausted all the patience he had in reserve. "Have you seen my wife?"

"I have."

"Did she eat something that did not agree with her?" He turned and demanded, "Where is she?"

His mama came to stand directly in front of him. "I beg you to remember I'm the one who endured ten hours of labor to bring you into this world."

"Mama, please..."

"I'm merely the messenger. Bronwyn bid me to tell you that while she loves you, she believes it was a mistake for the two of you to marry, and she has set off to arrange an annulment."

"An annulment!" Landon roared. Impossible. They were well and truly married, and there was no way a judge would grant her a divorce. Rarely did he let this anger surface, but this... this was too much. "Why did you not stop her? Talk sense into her."

"My boy, by now, I'd hoped you'd have learned that you simply can't tell someone what to believe. They..."

Landon finished the familiar advice. "They have to form their own opinions."

His wise mama wrapped her arms about his waist, and he rested his chin on the top of her head. Leaning back, his mama said, "Bronwyn doesn't deem herself worthy. I know you, Theo, and Mary have all tried in your own unique ways to assist her and attempted to make her see the fine qualities we know she possesses. But Bronwyn has yet to realize her own strengths. You, my dear boy, will need to employ two of your own greatest traits—patience and understanding."

Before inheriting the litany of responsibilities from his uncle, Landon wouldn't have agreed with his mama that those were his finer qualities. It was from his mama that he learned the art of patience.

She blessed him with one of her understanding smiles. "Do you remember when you were little and you would stomp inside, winded after racing about the estate with your cousin Baldwin?"

"Why, of course, I do. While Baldwin was able to jump and run about, I was left heaving air as if it was my last breath. It was terribly frustrating."

"And what did I tell you?"

"Play at your own pace, not others. I fail to see how that is of use to me now."

"You are not your papa. I believe your impetus to marry was out of fear. Stop pushing so hard. You chose wisely, but you gave Bronwyn no forewarning."

His mama was right as usual. "What am I to do?"

She patted his arm. "Give her time. She loves you. I have no qualms about that."

"How can you be so certain? She's gone and left me."

His mama raised her hand to cup his cheek. "In the few days I've spent with my daughter-in-law, there is one thing I know about her: she is fiercely independent. If she didn't love you, she'd never be willing to ask for assistance. Bronwyn needs to figure out who it is she truly wishes to be for herself. Not for her parents. Not for the good of the Network. Not even for you. The only way for her to achieve that is for Bronwyn to love and believe in herself." She gave him a pat on the cheek and stood back to stare at him.

"I suppose you're going to tell me if I truly love Bronwyn, I'll not hunt her down."

"No, silly boy, have you not been listening? I *said* give her time. Never did I say anything about space. You are her husband. It is your duty to protect her, even from herself."

Damn women and their riddles. Landon ran his hand

through his hair and kneaded the muscles in the back of his neck. It was the second time that day a woman had accused him of not listening. "What exactly do you suggest I do?"

"First, we are going back to the dining room. Second, you will simultaneously announce that you are wed while apologizing for Bronwyn's inability to return due to illness. Third, you will sit and endure Prinny's ramblings. Lastly, I will speak with Theo and arrange for your departure first thing in the morn."

Most people would describe his mama as quiet and meek. But in fact, she was Wellington's equal if not superior when it came to leading her family.

Landon leaned in for one more reassuring hug before winging his arm. He turned to address the footman who was busy eyeing the ceiling. "Larry, once we reach the dining room, please do the honor of escorting my mama to Bronwyn's seat."

The trio marched down the hall. A hush descended as they entered the dining room.

Landon walked to stand next to Archbroke, who garnered everyone's attention by clinking his fork against his glass.

Clearing his throat, Landon stood tall and said, "Unfortunately, most of you will not be granted the pleasure of my wife's company tonight as she has fallen ill. I anticipate a quick recovery, and we shall extend invitations upon our return to town."

Per his mama's instructions, he was to endure the rest of the evening. However, he was always a defiant child pushing boundaries. "I bid you all a good eve." With a decisive nod, he left the room. He didn't need his mama to arrange his departure plans. At four-and-thirty, he was quite capable of making the arrangements himself.

His chest constricted as he marched down the hall to his chamber. He needed Bronwyn - without her, his breathing became labored. With his hand on the latch of the door, Landon paused as he recited his plan. Locate his errant wife, ensure her safety, and exercise patience. It was a sound plan, and he was more than capable of enduring any anxiety he might experience while he waited for Bronwyn to learn to love herself as much as he loved her.

CHAPTER TWENTY-TWO

A silver button flew through the air and hit Bronwyn on the top of her shoulder.

"Ow." She rubbed her upper arm and glared at her best friend. Emma's dart-throwing skills meant she was extremely accurate and never missed her intended target. The metal button would leave a mark. Typical Emma. Her friend lived by the adage *actions speak louder than words*. Bronwyn sighed. Emma was right. It was time for Bronwyn to seek out her dad and receive the mark of a PORF.

"Will ye stop yer day dreamin' and help me out." Emma huffed, and a bolt of shimmering silver material landed on the cutting table before Bronwyn.

Bronwyn winced as she stretched out her arm to reach for the edge of the material. She had arrived back in town three days ago. Her first day back, Emma allowed her to remain abed and weep. But on the second, before the first rays of light hit the ground, Emma had hauled

Bronwyn out of bed and set her to work sorting buttons. It had taken three hours of monotonous labor and soul searching for Bronwyn to admit she didn't want an annulment. At a loss for what action to take next, Bronwyn had spent the rest of the day performing whatever mindless task Emma set for her.

Bronwyn unwound the material and aligned it against the yardstick. "What will you make out of this?"

"A gown, ye goose." Emma stood back with the shears in her hand. "Wot are ye goin' to do?"

"As soon as you've cut the silk loose, I'll pin the pattern."

"I'm not talkin' about the blasted gown." Emma shook her head. "Did gettin' hitched make ye daft?"

Glaring at her best friend, Bronwyn retorted, "Who ye callin' daft?" She was clearly at her wit's end, for her brash cockney accent had returned. Taking a deep breath, she gathered her thoughts and said, "You don't understand. Landon needs..."

"Bronwyn Cadby Neale." Emma snipped a slit into the material. "Ye can just stop yer blathering right now." The sharp blades snapped together, punctuating Emma's statement. "It's been three days, and ye have yet to come to ye senses." She ran the sharp shears down the material, slicing it away from the bolt. "I'll tell ye, I've considered knocking ye over the head with the chamber pot a time or two, to see if it'll help. But I think it better I use me words this time." Emma stuck her shears into her apron and put her hands on her hips. "Me best friend is no coward. This time tell me the truth—why did ye leave Lord Archbroke's estate in the middle of supper?"

Bronwyn blinked. She'd never mentioned to Emma the details of her departure. The blasted Network rumor mill was far too efficient. Grabbing the pattern that laid next to the table, she began pinning the translucent paper to the glorious silver silk. She wasn't ready to admit the truth: she had run away like a peagoose.

Emma crossed her arms over her chest and huffed. "If ye won't tell me, I'll tell ye wot I think."

Bronwyn pricked her finger as she mumbled, "I'm sure nothing will stop you either."

"Ye are bleedin', step away from me gown afore you ruin it." Emma rounded the table and, with her hip bumped Bronwyn out of the way. "Ye've never been good at needlepoint, but ye are smart, hardworking, and generous. And I'll tell ye, that's wot Lord Hadfield needs." Spinning the material around to affix the pattern to the other side, Emma paused and then added, "Wot do ye see in the mirror when ye look into one?"

Finally, a question Bronwyn was able to answer. "A woman with mouse brown hair, blue eyes, and of average looks."

Emma rolled her eyes. "That's not wot I see when I look at ye."

"Oh, really. Don't let me stop you. Pray tell, *what do you see*, Ms. Lennox?" The devil in Bronwyn spurred her to address her best friend by her formal name, knowing that Emma hated it.

"I see Countess Hadfield."

Touché. No one but Emma could get the best of Bronwyn.

Bronwyn conceded. "I'm not like the ladies Landon considers worthy to call close friends. Theo is brilliant, Mary is unique, and Lady Lucy, well, all the blasted rumors of how delightful and daring she is are all well and true." She leaned against the table and continued, "I'll tell you who I *used* to see in the looking glass. A Network elder's daughter, who wanted only to prove to everyone that she was worthy to succeed her dad and hold a seat at the council table."

"Ye were always too smart for ye own good." Placing the lid on the pins, Emma tugged Bronwyn over to the sitting area and plopped onto the settee. "Ye don't think I too worry about the day I'm to take me mum's place? That I don't wonder if I'm worthy of sittin' at the council table. I'm not smart like ye. I'm a darn seamstress. How do I know wot is best for the Network? But it is a great honor to represent one's family, and I'll muddle along. At least I'll have ye there next to me. Wait, if ye are a PORF, will ye still be on the council? Oh Gawd, don't say Harold will be sittin' next to me instead."

Bronwyn couldn't contain her laughter at Emma's appalled expression. "Don't worry, I'll be by your side at the council table—not representing the Cadby family but as a PORF." Wrapping her arms about her best friend, Bronwyn said, "You are too clever by half, and you don't even know it, Emma Lennox. I've been overthinking the matter. My heart belongs to one man, and I'm honored to be his wife. As for the rest, I'll follow your lead and simply muddle through it all. And as long as I have your aid and support, all will be well."

"Ye're daft to ask. I support ye, not because I pledged an oath, but because ye are the most amazing lady I know."

Bronwyn smiled and arched a brow. "Really? What of Theo or Mary or Lady Lucy or Lady Grace?"

With a pointed look, Emma replied, "I've seen all of them naked, inside and out. None of them are as perfect as ye believe them to be." Emma tilted her head and grinned. "Hmm... I reckon they are more like ye than me, tough on the outside but pure mush on the inside."

"And what are you?" Bronwyn teased.

"Aww... ye know, I'm hard on the outside and in. I've no time for love, which is wot turned all of ye ladies to mush."

"Emma Lennox, you're brilliant!"

Love had been Bronwyn's downfall. Not her love for Landon, but her lack of respect and care for herself. She needed to be the best person she could be, not what she thought others required her to be. Squeezing Emma's hand, Bronwyn said, "You know, the next time I see my reflection in a looking glass, I'll be seeing an entirely different person."

Peyton peeked out from the backroom and brought in a tray of tea and biscuits. She looked to Bronwyn and asked, "Should I go and prepare for our return home?"

"Aye." Bronwyn reached for the teapot, but Emma grasped the handle first.

"I think Willa and I will enjoy a nice cup of tea while

ye pay a visit to yer dad." Emma poured two cups of tea and motioned for Peyton to join her. Glancing at Bronwyn, Emma said, "Make sure ye choose a spot that won't interfere with me designs."

Bronwyn rose and said, "Aye, Ms. Lennox. I'll do just that."

Peyton giggled. "She's been practicing that hoity-toity voice those ladies use."

"By Jove, I reckon Bronwyn's managed to master it. Five shillings says she'll master the rest."

"I'll not be givin' you me hard-earned money." Peyton raised her teacup to her lips with her little finger sticking straight out.

"I'm still standing here," Bronwyn said.

Emma and Peyton clicked teacups and laughed. After a long moment, her best friend wiped her eyes and cleared her throat. "Give yer family me regards. And tell yer mum I'll not miss Sunday dinner this week. Now that I've rid meself of me guests, I'll be free again."

Dismissed by Emma, Bronwyn stomped to the door. Once she received the mark, would Emma dare to treat her the same? Bronwyn certainly hoped so, for who else would ensure she had her head screwed on the right way? The bell tinkled as Bronwyn left Emma's store. Intending to walk to her dad's store, she startled when Larry appeared in front of her. The footman motioned to a coach, which bore the Archbroke crest.

Bronwyn accepted Larry's assistance and stepped into the coach. Facing her cousin-in-law, she asked, "How long have you been out here waiting?"

"A while." Theo shifted to make room for Bronwyn on the forward-facing seat. "Where to, Lady Bronwyn?"

Theo had called her by her title, which meant she was not in the woman's good graces. "I was on my way to my dad's shop." Settling on to the cushioned bench, Bronwyn was oddly relieved to have Theo accompany her. "Does Landon know you are here?"

"Your husband is aware of your whereabouts."

Theo neatly evaded her question and answered the one Bronwyn had wanted to ask.

Theo smoothed out nonexistent wrinkles from her gown. "Landon arrived in London a few hours after you. Unfortunately, it took Archbroke a whole day to settle Prinny's feathers enough to convince the man to leave so we too could be here in town for you." Theo leaned out the window and yelled, "Cadby's."

Once the coach was in full motion, Bronwyn asked, "How did your husband calm the Prince Regent?"

"Archbroke can be extremely persuasive if he chooses to. Plus, after we discussed the matter, Archbroke had no qualms settling matters with the Prince Regent." Theo patted Bronwyn's arm and then settled her hands in her lap.

Confused by Theo's comforting gesture, Bronwyn asked, "But how?"

Theo drew back the window curtain and peered out onto the crowded street. Bronwyn's dad's shop wasn't far, but the coach was barely moving. "Hereditary peers will always hold a majority seat..."

"Peers? What does the number of hereditary peers have to do with my marriage to Landon?"

Theo swiveled to face her. "Nothing. But it is the reason why Prinny decided to invite himself to stay at Archbroke manor."

Fustian. Bronwyn wanted to smack herself with a chamber pot. Christopher had harped on at her endlessly for making assumptions before completing a full inquiry. Head bowed, Bronwyn said, "I'm sorry for leaving and disrupting your lovely supper."

Bronwyn waited for a lecture, but Theo reached for her hand. "You must promise to never leave in darkness again. You had me terribly worried. We were all worried until we received word from Mrs. Barnwell that you were safe. Landon, especially."

"He knows I've been staying with Emma?"

"Of course; he'd not leave you unprotected."

"But I..."

"You needed time." Theo squeezed her hand tightly. "Landon understands." The coach came to a complete stop. Her cousin's kind and concerned eyes searched Bronwyn's face. "Would you like for me to accompany you inside? Landon shared his experience receiving the mark. It did not sound at all pleasant."

"My dad has placed the PORF mark upon all the ladies who have married into the line. It is said to be nothing compared to childbirth." Bronwyn eyed Theo's rounded stomach. "But if you would like to stay and keep my mum company while I receive the mark, so she doesn't worry overly much, I'd appreciate it."

With a nod, Theo stood and exited the coach. As Larry assisted Bronwyn, Theo said, "Landon is like a brother rather than a cousin to me. I know you already have three younger sisters, but I've never had a sister, and I'd be honored if you would..."

Bronwyn hugged Theo in front of all and sundry on the front stoop of her dad's shop, not caring that it was a breach of etiquette. "I've always wanted an older sister." Grinning from ear to ear, Bronwyn led Theo around the back to the family entrance. They were immediately greeted and engulfed by multiple arms. Her mum, brothers, and sisters all took a turn embracing Bronwyn and then their newest member to the family, Theo.

Bronwyn obediently followed her dad into the backroom of the store where his tools were hidden. She sat in the same chair Landon had when he received the mark and carefully arranged her skirts. The silence ate away at her courage.

Instruments and ink at the ready, her dad asked, "Where would you like for me to place the mark?"

Emma's taunting words echoed through her mind. Bronwyn smirked and pointed to the spot where the button had hit her shoulder—it would be a test for Emma to design dresses and gowns that would hide her mark, but her best friend would rise to the challenge.

Her dad didn't challenge her decision, merely looked at her with wide eyes and shook his head. "Ye're a stubborn one." He poured a dark amber liquid into a glass. "But I love ye." Her dad handed her the tumbler and said, "Here, drink this before I start."

An hour later, a slightly tipsy Bronwyn descended the stairs. She was officially a PORF. Oddly, she didn't feel any different. She slumped to the kitchen bench and rested her head on her arms.

Her dad said, "Tell her husband we'll watch over her tonight and tend to her bandages."

It was good to know she was still welcome under her parents' roof. She'd go home on the morrow, as soon as the world stopped spinning.

CHAPTER TWENTY-THREE

*T*he sound of footmen dragging trunk after trunk down the main staircase echoed down the hallway. The drawing room occupants, Waterford, Mary, and Christopher, all of whom had accompanied Landon back to London, remained silent.

For three days, from sunup to sundown, Landon remained rooted next to the window looking out onto the street. Waiting patiently for his wife to return. If it hadn't been for his silent companions in the room, he'd not have eaten or managed to keep a hold on his sanity. When Bronwyn had failed to return to their townhouse or appear at her parents' lodgings, Landon panicked. But Waterford eased his worries by reminding him that the Network would not fail to protect his wife. As a council member, Waterford was apprised of all activity, and only an hour after their return to London, a messenger had confirmed Bronwyn was safely tucked into a cot above Emma's store. The uncertainty over how long it might be before Landon saw his wife again gnawed at his patience.

Tearing himself from the window for a moment, Landon asked his younger brother, "Why the sudden decision to relocate today?"

Christopher's eyes darted to Mary, who was sitting in one of the leather chairs by the fire, and then retorted, "What makes you believe I hadn't planned the move for this day?"

Mary sat unnaturally still. Since midmorning, the woman had exuded an edginess that worried Landon. It wasn't that Landon hadn't expected Christopher to move into lodgings of his own. He was fully aware his brother wanted to spread his wings. After all, it was he who had located and facilitated Christopher's purchase of the townhouse within walking distance of their law offices. Of course, no one knew of his involvement except for the owner from whom Christopher purchased the property.

Landon turned back to stare out the window. Christopher's trunks were being systematically loaded into a lorry that was already half full.

Landon asked, "I'm fully aware you had made preparations to acquire and relocate to your own bachelor lodgings. However..." He left his vantage point by the window and walked to the sideboard. As he passed by Mary, the woman's lips curled into a pleasant smile. Whatever Mary was about, a drink would help fortify his shot nerves. Splashing a healthy portion of brandy into a tumbler, he continued, "With Bronwyn away—why the rush to move today?"

Christopher moved to the spot Landon had vacated moments before. "Looks to be a rather fine day. No clouds. A perfect day to transport my things." His brother spun and rushed to the door. Christopher strolled, never rushed. He'd have to interrogate Christopher later, but right now Landon's priority was to wait for his errant wife to return.

As Christopher opened the door to leave, he paused. Halfway out, his brother smiled and said, "I'd love to stay and keep you company, but there is a stack of files awaiting me at the office. Your jaunt to Scotland has set me back. In addition, it's been challenging to find another assistant as competent as my last. Alas, I shall be buried in casework."

Christopher's speech sounded like one of his well-rehearsed closing statements. His complaint regarding it being a challenge to find a new assistant was highly peculiar. Landon himself had reviewed the list of interviewees prior to this departure for Gretna Green. He ensured every candidate was more than qualified for the position. He continued to ponder his brother's monologue when Mary mumbled the word *alone*.

Landon glanced at Mary. "I apologize, were you speaking to me?"

The couple had appeared on the steps of his townhouse at the crack of dawn. Waterford's lame excuse of an accident involving a broken stove in their kitchens and of his need for a good hearty breakfast didn't hold water, but he hadn't pressed for details.

Mary raised her voice a tad louder and replied, "I said —it'll be quiet here, with you all alone."

The woman was up to no good. Her gaze skirted his. Mary was a terrible liar.

Landon stalked back to the window. But his attention wasn't on Christopher coordinating the last-minute details of his move outside, it was concentrated on the shadowed reflection of Mary and Waterford. The couple was making the most amusing gestures behind his back as they tried to communicate in silence. It was apparent they were not in agreement whatever it was they were discussing.

He cleared his throat and turned to face them. "I forgot to inform Christopher that I wish for him to accompany me to Harrington's dinner party tomorrow eve." Landon briskly headed for the door. "I shall return in a moment."

Closing the door behind him, Landon stepped in place and then lightened his footfalls to mimic his leaving. With his eyes closed and an ear pressed to the wood, Landon tried to decipher the couple's conversation.

The scent of daisies set his heart pounding. "Eavesdropping is a terrible habit." He stood frozen at Bronwyn's sweet, teasing whisper. He'd wished for three long days Bronwyn would magically appear. What if he opened his eyes, and it was his imagination playing tricks on him?

Slowly opening his eyes, he suppressed the bubble of laughter as he took in the sight of his wife bent at the waist facing him with her ear pressed against the door.

With her blue eyes sparkling up at him, Bronwyn said, "Mary sounds rather anxious today, wouldn't you say?"

He cupped her flushed cheek. "You're here."

Bronwyn straightened and stepped closer, pressing him back against the drawing-room door. He ran his thumb over the dark circles under her eye. "You're home."

She planted her hands on his chest and rose on to her tiptoes to lightly press her lips against his. Elation flowed throughout him as he wrapped both arms around her waist and pulled her tighter to him. His wife's tongue traced his lower lip before she deepened the kiss.

Thank goodness the door behind him supported his weight. His knees nearly buckled as his wife's hand roamed lower to cup his rigid cock.

She released his mouth. "I'm happy to see you too."

The door opened, and they toppled to the drawing-room floor. "Oomph."

With Bronwyn atop of him, he wished Waterford and Mary could magically *dis*appear.

"Oh my!" Mary stood over them with a hand over her mouth. The mirth in her chocolate eyes evident. "Husband, I think best if we take our leave now."

Landon remained flat on the floor as Bronwyn scrambled to her feet and embraced Mary. "I've missed you!"

"I suspect not at much as you missed your husband." Mary giggled. "And definitely not as much as he missed you. Shall I return for tea?"

Before either Bronwyn or Landon could answer,

Waterford said, "I believe Lady Bronwyn will be other-wise disposed this afternoon. Plus, I have plans for us today."

"What plans?" Mary asked.

Waterford replied, "I'm taking you shopping."

Mary gave Bronwyn one last squeeze and then turned to her husband. "Are we going to visit the apothe-cary?" At Waterford's nod, Mary smiled and waved goodbye over her shoulder.

As soon as the couple had disappeared, Bronwyn asked, "Why did Mary look excited to visit the apothecary?"

Landon rose to his feet and chuckled. "If I had to guess, they are off to buy more French letters."

"Whatever for?"

"They have decided not to have children." Landon grabbed Bronwyn's hand and drew her over to the settee. "No need to frown. Waterford agreed to the arrangement before they married."

Bronwyn released his hand and adjusted her skirts as she asked, "But Waterford is an earl; what of the title?"

"The earldom shall pass to his cousin, who is a fair sort."

"But what of the Network?" Bronwyn sat, and when Landon did the same, she added. "Who will succeed him on the council?"

Landon reached for her hands that were clasped tightly in her lap. "Do you believe it fair that the council be comprised of a select few families and designated by lineage? With the departure of Tobias, Lord Burke, to

America, I'm faced with the dilemma that the Protection of the Royal Family is limited to two families, instead of three."

Bronwyn's brows slanted down into a deep frown. "You are talking of rules and traditions established long ago. Are you considering altering how things have been done for generations?"

"As the holder of the rondure, I could, but I'll not abuse the power and authority that has been granted to me." Landon couldn't resist. He leaned forward and pulled her onto his lap before continuing. "There must have been a reason why events led to the rondure resurfacing after all these years." Landon searched his wife's features and settled his gaze upon her intelligent eyes. "I've spent many months considering the why, what and how, with little success. I suspect the answer requires more than pure logic. It was one of the reasons why I decided to propose to you."

Wide-eyed Bronwyn said, "I don't understand. You didn't even know my affiliation to the Network when you proposed."

He shook his head. "You still haven't fully grasped your worth." He leaned down to whisper, "Your keen mind was but one of the reasons why I chose you for wife." Nibbling on her ear, he confessed, "I married the woman who captured my heart and compels me to live without fear but with faith that matters will be resolved. I merely need to be patient."

CHAPTER TWENTY-FOUR

*B*ronwyn shifted in her husband's lap as his lips left her ear. She inhaled deeply. Finally, the tension she had held in her bones these past few weeks eased. Home. Landon was her home and her safe space. She whispered, "And my heart belongs to you." Landon tightened his hold on her, but she placed a hand on his muscled chest, holding him at bay. "I apologize for my hasty departure from Theo's lovely supper."

Landon lifted her chin with a knuckle. "Forget about the dinner. Are you certain your heart belongs to me?"

"Without a doubt." Sheepishly, she met Landon's eyes. "After three days of hard contemplation." Landon's dimple appeared, and she bolstered her courage with another deep breath. "I have a few confessions to make."

Landon's hazel eyes were trained solely upon her. "Before you do, I have a couple of revelations I'd like to share with you first. If you don't mind."

Staring at her husband's lips, Bronwyn slid her arm

up and about Landon's neck and pressed herself close. She wanted to taste the lips that she had dreamt of kissing her intimately. She needed to feel them pressed against her neck. Tilting her head, she leaned in.

Landon placed a finger upon her lips, preventing the kiss she longed for.

"If we kiss, I'll not want to stop until I have you atop me, riding me—hard."

The intensity of his gaze set her blood to boil. Heat and desire pooled at her core.

There were truths she promised herself she would no longer withhold from Landon. She needed to clear them from her conscience.

Bronwyn leaned back slightly, leaving her hand on the back of his neck where her fingers stroked his skin. "What are these revelations you want to share with me?"

Eyes shut, Landon said, "Eight years ago, when you walked into my office, I had doubts that a girl from the east side would be wise enough to fill the position of legal assistant."

"I, too, had concerns."

At her admission he asked, "Is that so? I'd have never guessed, for I distinctly remember you brazenly standing before me and claiming there was no one else better suited for the position."

"At the time, I wasn't referring to the role of being your assistant. I was speaking of the importance of someone within the Network keeping an eye on you."

Landon's face became dangerously expressionless. "Explain."

Taking a moment to arrange her thoughts, she placed both hands in her lap and interlocked her fingers. "The Network elders deemed it imperative someone be assigned to your protection as long as you were unmarked. They deemed the probability of you inheriting high, given the tendency of men in the Neale family to leave this earth well before their time. I petitioned for the position and was granted the honor of being assigned to you. I had no idea what was expected of a legal assistant."

Landon's features transformed from a frown into a knowing grin. "Yet you excelled. And that is why I know you will be a wonderful countess."

Grinning, Bronwyn said, "That is the same conclusion I arrived at. Except it took days of sorting buttons and..." Her body shook with a shiver. "And mending, to figure it out."

"I have one more confession." Landon's arm tightened about her waist as if he feared she might flee. "While I was traveling abroad with Mary and Waterford, I realized I'd subconsciously fallen in love with you and simultaneously been callous toward your feelings for me."

Bronwyn couldn't help but stiffen as she asked, "You knew I'd fallen in love with you?"

"For six years, I assumed I was misinterpreting the subtle lingering looks and undercurrents. I persuaded myself that your feelings for me were purely platonic." Landon placed a chaste kiss upon her cheek. "When Mary accused me of already being in love with another, I couldn't deny it any longer."

A knot twisted in her stomach. "Tell me, when did Mary make this accusation?"

"It was while I..." Her husband cleared his throat once more. Not a good sign. Unblinking, he said, "Amidst my attempt to convince her to consider my suit." He quickly continued, "It was the honorable and right thing to do, and I hoped it would spur Waterford to act."

"You did not know they were already betrothed?"

"You did?"

"Aye, the Network is well informed. Waterford signed the betrothal papers before he left for the Continent." Bronwyn frowned. "You had already received the mark. How is it Archbroke did not inform you of these details prior to your departure—unless you were not forthcoming with your own plans."

She had guessed correctly; guilt was plastered across Landon's features. Bronwyn placed a chaste kiss upon his cheek and whispered into his ear, "It's a good thing you married me. This way, I can prevent you from making such mistakes in the future."

Before she could pull back, Landon's lips fastened on her neck. The rogue was going to leave yet another mark. She didn't care, she let out a moan.

The pressure of his lips lightened. Landon asked, "Any other confessions?"

"Two." She wanted to be done conversing. His teasing lips had her rushing to get the words out. "I agreed to marry you because I loved you all those years you were a barrister but also because..." She took a deep breath. "I honestly didn't believe I had a choice despite your reassurances."

Landon ceased kissing her. No longer crushed to his body, the additional three inches of space he placed between them felt like a vast chasm. "You didn't believe me?"

Bronwyn tried to edge closer, but for every inch she moved forward, Landon moved back. She wrung her hands in her lap. "Not until I left, and you didn't come after me."

She regretted the hurt that resided in the depths of his eyes. Bowing her head, she continued her attempt at explaining her thoughts. "I realized it was entirely my decision if I wished to remain married to you—and I do. I've fallen in love with you. Not a barrister. Not an earl. Not the head PORF, but with the man who is amazingly patient, caring, and is..." Despite the heaviness in her heart, her lips curled into a smile as she added, "An excellent lover."

He lifted her chin. "And your other admission?"

She blinked. "I've another?" Her brow furrowed into a frown.

"You said you had two." The mischievous twinkle in his eyes reappeared.

Tilting her head, Bronwyn answered, "Aye. I love you, and I want to be your wife."

He crushed his lips to hers. She threw her arms over his shoulders and about his neck. Her skirts tangled and twisted as she struggled to shift her legs in an attempt to straddle him. Landon's hands moved down to her waist, and he lifted her with him as he stood.

What was he doing? He'd said earlier he wanted her atop, straddling him—her favorite position.

The hem of her dress inched up her leg, the material bunching in Landon's hand. With her legs freed from the material, she wrapped them around his waist.

Winding her fingers in his hair, she said, "I want to make love with you."

Landon lowered both hands to rest on the underside of her bottom. "Loosen your hold on me, love."

She obeyed. Landon lowered her until her hands interlocked behind his neck. How many more positions were possible? Her husband was constantly introducing her to new possibilities, playing havoc with her preferences.

The stiff material of his falls grazed against her core as he ground his hips to hers. She needed him inside of her. She slid her right hand down Landon's glorious chest and stomach, basking in the way his muscles always twitched beneath her touch. It was a heady experience she would never tire of.

He shifted to allow space for her hand to slip between them and unfasten his buttons. Bronwyn stroked Landon's erect shaft as it sprung free. He groaned in her ear as his cock increased in size. The anticipation of having him in her was torture. Finally, he lifted her higher and she positioned his tip at her entrance. She released her hold on him as he lowered her inch by inch, until he was deep inside of her. Incapable of rational thought, she moaned her delight. Her pleasure mounted. Landon set a leisurely pace, long slow strokes in and out. Impatient to find her release, she repositioned her hands to his shoulders to gain additional leverage. She increased the tempo. Landon's breathing became labored, and a burst of worry broke through her dazed mind.

Breathlessly, she asked, "Are you well?" Bronwyn slowed but did not cease her movements. "Should we stop?"

"No." He pumped into her long and hard. "I'm well."

She didn't believe him. Bronwyn circled her hips, squeezing her thighs tight and lifting herself to plaster her chest to his. With the tip of his cock remaining inside her, she said, "Enjoyable, but you know what my preferences are."

"Remind me." Landon's voice was strained, and his stare held a challenge.

Fully aware verbal sparring and sharing her likes in detail heightened Landon's excitement, she ran her tongue along the edge of his ear. "I prefer it faster. Deeper. Harder." Bronwyn relaxed her arms and legs to take all of him in her again. With him deep inside, she flexed the muscles at her core.

"Minx, tell me what you want."

Landon loved clear and succinct answers. Adopting a no-nonsense tone, she said, "I need your hands free to pinch my nipples and slap my bum. I want to ride you."

"What if I suggest an alternative?" Desire and a hint of mischief filled Landon's eyes.

She leaned back. The movement caused his engorged

shaft to sink deeper, and she moaned as little waves of excitement rolled throughout her.

Licking her lips, she asked, "Will this new position satisfy all my requirements?"

"Hmm. Yes, I believe it will." Landon's fingers dug into her waist. He slid her higher and ordered, "Lower your legs."

She did as her husband instructed and unwrapped her legs from his waist. He lowered her until her feet were firmly planted back on the floor. Knees weak, she held onto Landon for support.

His hands glided up her over her ribs and down along her arms. He grabbed her wrists and brought them together. Holding her wrists with one hand, he stepped to the side. Landon positioned her hands to rest along the frame of the settee so she stood, bent at the waist. Her husband skimmed his hands over her back and said, "Don't remove your hands."

Landon disappeared from sight. Her hand lifted from the back of the settee as she turned to look over her shoulder. Landon lifted her skirts and, with one hand, held them in place, bunched at her waist. His other hand grazed over her right bottom cheek. She inhaled and waited for the fleeting sting of her husband's hand against her skin that would send moisture pooling between her legs. But Landon was in no rush.

His dimple appeared. "I told you not to move your hands."

Bronwyn's pulse raced at the devilish twinkle in her husband's eyes. She turned back around and replaced her hand where he had instructed to keep them in place. Instead of her husband's palm, the broad tip of Landon's hardened shaft slid down the crack between her bottom and then along her wet slit.

She released a deep, desire-filled moan. Bronwyn's eyes closed, and her head rolled forward. She wanted him inside of her. She rocked her bottom back toward him. His fingers dug into her hips. His cock filled her in one long, hard stroke—exactly the way she wanted him to. Bronwyn cried out in ecstasy.

Landon's hand roamed higher and snaked around to fondle her breast, bringing him deeper within her. Her rake of a husband circled his hips as he pinched her nipple. Shivers ran down the middle of her back. Her back arched, filling Landon's hand with her breast. He responded by giving it a hard squeeze as he began to pump hard into her.

He withdrew his hand. She wanted to plead for it to return but just as she was about to vocalize her wish, his palm slapped against her bottom and her inner muscles spasmed.

"Wife. Tell me..." Landon deepened his thrusts and quickened his pace.

Her fingers dug into the wood frame. "Landon, don't stop." On the verge of release, she began to rock back. The sound of their bodies joining pushed her over the edge. She inhaled and exhaled deeply she basked in the pleasure seeping into her muscles.

Landon continued to make love to her. The man was tireless. A tug on her scalp had her peaking a second time. *Blast*—she would never be able to claim a singular position as her favorite.

AFTER A RIGOROUS NIGHT of bed sport, Landon insisted they postpone breaking their fast in favor of a couple of hours of sleep. Now, well past the nooning hour, he was pleased to see his wife's beautiful face devoid of the dark smudges under her eyes. Folding the daily paper, Landon waited for Bronwyn to lift her cup of tea to her pretty lips. If she had a mouth full of liquid, she wouldn't be able to scold him for what he was about to share.

"I forgot to mention last evening that, prior to me leaving Archbroke's dinner, I announced our union and that we would be holding an official ball here to celebrate the occasion of your recovery."

Bronwyn's eyes widened briefly over the rim of her cup. "My recovery? What ailment did you give me?"

He chuckled and lifted his own cup filled with coffee. Thank goodness his wife had a sense of humor. "Nothing deadly." Before taking a sip, he added, "Theo and Mama have offered to assist you with the planning and organization."

"Splendid. That should keep them busy and out of my hair while I attend to matters at the office." Bronwyn sipped her tea and stared at him.

Landon managed to swallow the mouth full of the hot dark brew without sputtering. "Office? Do you mean you intend to return to work for Christopher?"

The corner of her lips twitched as she nodded. "Only while Christopher searches for a suitable replacement."

"Hmph. I suspect Christopher might be of a similar mind as I am. There is no one quite like you." Raising his cup to lips again, he added, "He'll never be satisfied with another." He took a long sip of his coffee.

"You know, Christopher really should receive the mark. In the meantime, I shall see to it that my replacement will be capable of meeting *all* of your brother's requirements. I'll have everything in place before I begin my lying in."

Coffee spewed from his mouth and flew across the table.

At his side in a flash, Bronwyn pounded on his back as he coughed and sputtered.

"You are *enceinte*?"

His wife let out a laugh as she rubbed his back. "No, silly. But I can't imagine it will be long before I am, given the frequency with which we engage in marital relations." One last giggle escaped her as she resumed her seat. "Do I have your permission to assist Christopher?"

"Wife, you don't need my permission as to how you go about your day. Do as you wish. I merely ask you reserve the evenings for me."

Bronwyn tilted her head, pursed her lips, and with a decisive nod, said, "I suppose that is a reasonable request. I have a similar one of my own. Will you agree to spend Saturdays with me?"

"All day?"

"Yes—*all day* until I fulfill my duty and birth a son."

"Hmm…" What a wonderful future he had to look forward to. Revealing his dimple, Landon asked, "And if we are only blessed with girls?"

"Then you shall be spending many a Saturday with your wife."

He winked and nodded. "You, my dear, are a tough negotiator. I agree."

Thank you for reading Revealing a Rogue.
Next - Book 2: Tempting a Gentleman

ALSO BY RACHEL ANN SMITH -
HISTORICAL

THE HADFIELDS

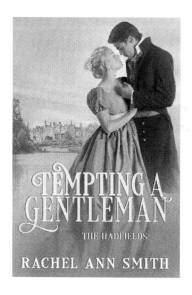

Book 2: Tempting a Gentleman

She runs a successful dress shop.

He's a talented barrister.

Will his skills as a lover or as a lawyer prevail?

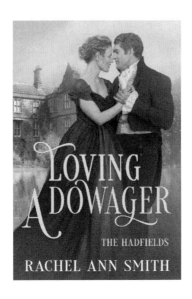

Book 3: Loving a Dowager

Will Henrietta Neale, the Dowager of Hadfield, reject the suit of a younger man or will she give love a second chance?

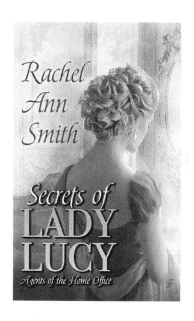

Book 1: Secrets of Lady Lucy

She is determined to foil an attempted kidnapping.

He is set on discovering her secrets.

When the ransom demand comes due—will it be for Lady Lucy's heart?

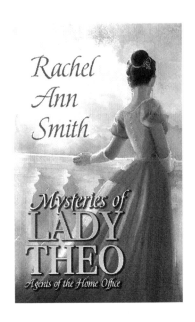

Book 2: Mysteries of Lady Theo

She inherited her family's duty to the Crown.

His duty to the Crown took priority.

Will the same duty that forced them together be what
ultimately drives them apart?

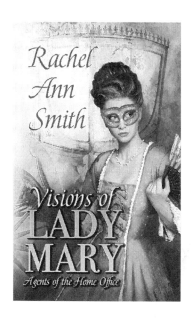

Book 3: Visions of Lady Mary

She wants a life of adventure.

He once called her a witch.

Will fate prevail or will Mary's stubbornness win out?

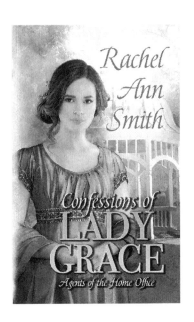

Book 4: Confessions of Lady Grace

She sacrificed her future to save his life.

He survived only to return home and find she is
betrothed to another.

Will her confessions set them both free?